CHRISTMAS IN MY HEART®

18

JOE L. WHEELER

Christmas 2009

With love to
Martha
on behalf of
Michelle
Strangely enough,
our fondest Christmas memories
are generally tied to tough times

Annapolis, Maryland

Pacific Press® Publishing Association
Nampa, Idaho
Oshawa, Ontario, Canada
www.pacificpress.com

Copyright © 2009 by
Joe L. Wheeler
All rights reserved
Printed in the United States of America

Cover design by Steve Lanto
Cover art by vintageart.com
Interior illustrations from the library of Joe L. Wheeler
Inside design by Aaron Troia

The author assumes full responsibility for the accuracy of all facts and quotations as cited in this book.

Christmas in My Heart® is a registered trademark of Joe L. Wheeler and may not be used by anyone else in any form. Visit Joe Wheeler's Web site at www .joewheelerbooks.com. Representing the author is WordServe Literary Group, Ltd., 10152 Knoll Circle, Highland Ranch, CO 80130.

Additional copies of this book are available by calling toll-free 1-800-765-6955 or by visiting www.adventistbookcenter.com.

Library of Congress Cataloging-in-Publication Data:

Wheeler, Joe L., 1936-   comp.
    Christmas in my heart. Book 18.

    1. Christmas stories, American. I. Title:
Christmas in my heart. Book 18.

ISBN 13: 978-0-8163-2360-9
ISBN 10: 0-8163-2360-7

09 10 11 12 13 • 5 4 3 2 1

Dedication

As I look back through the years to that unnumbered white *Christmas in My Heart*® book with its Currier & Ives cover, it seems like it was a long time ago. As book series go, since so few last more than a few years, it *has* been a long time. Eighteen Christmases, to be exact.

And he was there back at the beginning. There to interview me on "Saturday Seminar" on radio station WGTS (now one of the leading Christian radio stations in America). Each year that has followed, he has once again brought his growing audience up-to-date in terms of all of our books. Every November, we share the airwaves together. I'm comfortable now—it's like home when the hour-long broadcast is taped—but it was not so at the beginning: I all but died on the air.

Somehow, he forgave me for my stage fright and had me back a year later.

So this Christmas, it is indeed fitting that this cherished friend (one of the most beloved radio interviewers of the Washington, D.C. Metroplex), a radio host who has had so much to do with our series' success, a man who (like me) chokes up when discussing or retelling deeply moving stories—well, what a joy it is to dedicate *Christmas in My Heart* 18 (our seventieth book) to

DR. GERRY FULLER
of
SILVER SPRING, MARYLAND.

Books by Joe L. Wheeler

Abraham Lincoln: A Man of Faith and Courage
Best of Christmas in My Heart 1
Best of Christmas in My Heart 2
Candle in the Forest and Other Christmas Stories Children
 Love
Christmas in My Heart®, books 1–17
Christmas in My Heart Treasuries (4)
Christmas in My Heart, audio books 1–6
Christmas in My Soul, gift books (3)
Dick, the Babysitting Bear and Other Great Wild Animal
 Stories
Easter in My Heart
Everyday Heroes
Great Stories Remembered, I, II, III
Great Stories Remembered, audio books I–III
Great Stories Remembered Classic Books (12 books)
Heart to Heart Stories of Dads
Heart to Heart Stories of Moms
Heart to Heart Stories of Friendship
Heart to Heart Stories for Grandparents
Heart to Heart Stories of Love
Heart to Heart Stories for Sisters
Heart to Heart Stories of Teachers
Owney, the Post Office Dog and Other Great Dog Stories
Remote Controlled
Smoky, the Ugliest Cat in the World and Other Great Cat
 Stories

Spot, the Dog That Broke the Rules and Other Great Heroic
 Animal Stories
St. Nicholas: A Closer Look at Christmas
Soldier Stories
Stories of Angels
Tears of Joy for Mothers
The Twelve Stories of Christmas
Time for a Story
What's So Good About Tough Times?
Wildfire, the Red Stallion and Other Great Horse Stories
Wings of God, The
Zane Grey's Impact on American Life and Letters

Acknowledgments

Epigraph: "A Cradle Hymn," by Isaac Watts. Published in R. H. Stoddard and F. F. Browne's *The Golden Treasury of Poetry and Prose* (New York: N. D. Thompson & Co., 1883). Original text owned by Joe Wheeler.

Introduction: "Simplicity at Christmas," by Joseph Leininger Wheeler. Copyright © 2008. Printed by permission of the author. All rights reserved.

"The Magic of the Season," by Isobel Stewart. Reprinted by permission of the author. All rights reserved.

"Oren's Christmas Present," by Idona Hill. If anyone can provide knowledge of the earliest publication of this old story or author's next of kin, please send to Joe Wheeler (P.O. Box 1246, Conifer, CO 80433).

"So This Is Christmas!" by Temple Bailey. If anyone can provide knowledge of the earliest publication of this old story or author's next of kin, please send to Joe Wheeler (P.O. Box 1246, Conifer, CO 80433).

"The Missionary Barrel," by Carolyn Abbot Stanley. If anyone can provide knowledge of the earliest publication of this old story or author's next of kin, please send to Joe Wheeler (P.O. Box 1246, Conifer, CO 80433).

"The Christmas Rose," by Marlene J. Chase. Published in *The War Cry*, December 1997. Reprinted by permission of the author.

"Through the Mike," by Ruth Herrick Myers. Published in *The Girl's Companion*, December 24, 1939. Text printed by permission of Joe Wheeler (P.O. Box 1246, Conifer, CO 80433) and David C. Cook, Colorado Springs, CO.

"One Christmas Eve," by Frank Bennett. Published in *Farm Journal*, December 1951. Reprinted by permission of Farm Journal Media.

"Grandma Thomas's Three Christmas Trees," by Jean Jeffrey Gietzen. Published in *Catholic Digest*, January 1985. Reprinted by permission of the author.

"An Exchange of Gifts," by Diane Rayner. Reprinted with permission from *Guideposts* magazine. Copyright © 1983 by *Guideposts*. All rights reserved. www.guideposts.com.

"Empty Heart," by Claire Jones. If anyone can provide knowledge of the earliest publication of this old story or author's next of kin, please send to Joe Wheeler (P.O. Box 1246, Conifer, CO 80433).

Contents

A Cradle Hymn

HUSH! my dear, lie still, and slumber,
    Holy angels guard thy bed!
Heavenly blessings without number
    Gently falling on thy head.

Sleep, my babe; thy food and raiment,
    House and home thy friends provide;
All without thy care or payment,
    All thy wants are well supplied.

How much better thou 'rt attended
    Than the Son of God could be,
When from heaven He descended,
    And became a child like thee.

Soft and easy is thy cradle:
    Coarse and hard thy Saviour lay:
When His birthplace was a stable,
    And His softest bed was hay.

See the kinder shepherds round Him,
    Telling wonders from the sky!

There they sought Him, there they found Him,
    With His virgin mother by.

See the lovely Babe a-dressing;
    Lovely Infant, how He smiled!
When He wept, the mother's blessing
    Soothed and hushed the holy Child.

Lo! He slumbers in His manger,
    Where the horned oxen fed;
Peace, my darling, here's no danger,
    Here's no ox anear thy bed.

Mayst thou live to know and fear Him,
    Trust and love Him all thy days;
Then go dwell forever near Him,
    See His face, and sing His praise!

I could give thee thousand kisses,
    Hoping what I most desire;
Not a mother's fondest wishes
    Can to greater joys aspire.
                                    —Isaac Watts

Simplicity at Christmas

Joseph Leininger Wheeler

Simple Gifts
" 'Tis a gift to be simple, 'tis the gift to be free,
'Tis the gift to come down where you ought to be,
And when we find ourselves in the place just right,
'Twill be in the valley of love and delight.
When true simplicity is gain'd,
To bow and to bend we shan't be asham'd,
To turn, turn will be our delight,
Till by turning, turning we come round right."
—Elder Joseph Brackett (1848)

What we owe the Shakers

It is almost impossible to discuss simplicity without referencing the millennial sect known to us as the Shakers. Their origins date back to 1747 with their Quaker roots in England. Since an original tenet was celibacy, the sect never got very large. Ann Lee (known as Mother Ann) brought eight of her followers to America in 1774, and settled near Watervliet, New York. From there the sect spread across the eastern states. Though their membership never got very large and they are virtually extinct today, the Shakers have had a disproportionate effect on the American mind.

During the early '90s, every autumn two other professors and I would take a busload of our students to New England, where we would "ride the fall colors down." Each year we'd visit the Shaker Village in Canterbury, Vermont. And each year the students' reactions would be the same: being themselves products of American affluence, they found it incredibly difficult to even imagine living in those big drafty wooden buildings, communally at that (men living in quarters separate from the women). How bitterly cold they must have been in the wintertime! The students also found it difficult to understand why anyone would volunteer to live in such stripped-down rooms. Personal possessions and furniture were spartan.

Scholars believe that "Simple Gifts," rather than being a hymn as it was long believed, was written to be sung during their communal folk dancing. Nevertheless, for the Shakers, all life had a spiritual dimension. Of them, *Encyclopedia Britannica* editors postulate, "The Shakers won the admiration of the world for their model farms, and orderly, prosperous communities. Their industry and ingenuity produced numerous (usually unpatented) inventions . . . (including the common clothespin). They were the first to package and market seeds and were once the largest producers of medicinal herbs. In exchanges with outsiders they were noted for their fair dealing. Shaker dances and songs are a genuine folk art, and the simple beauty, functionalism, and honest craftsmanship of their meeting houses, barns, and artifacts have had a lasting influence on American design."[1]

Let us keep the Shaker way of life in mind as we discuss ways in which we might restore simplicity and sanity to a Christmas season that many feel has lost its spiritual moorings.

Threatening to skip Christmas

Several days ago, as I was waiting in line to mail some Christmas packages, a woman behind me announced, "I think I'm going to skip Christmas this year! Kids just take, take, take—and nobody appreciates anything!"

The clerk at the counter smiled, "What kind of a bee got into your bonnet, Cathy?"

Calming down somewhat, the complainer said, "Well, maybe that's a rather extreme position to take. Most likely I won't *really* skip Christmas—but I'm fed up just the same."

"How's that?" queried the clerk.

"Well, I just wish Christmas hadn't been wrecked by being commercialized to death."

"You mean, I suppose," piped up another lugger of packages, "that you're comparing all this excess to a time when things were more serene and . . . uh—"

"*Simpler!* That's the word I was searching for. . . . When I was young, Christmas was so much simpler. Goodness knows we didn't get much back then—but what we got, we *cherished*. Not like today."

There was silence for a minute or two before the first speaker spoke again, "This Christmas, I think I'll spend all my Christmas money on birdseed and suet—oh yes, and chickens for the two adorable foxes that hang around our place," and righteously, "chickens, because we're not supposed to feed processed food to animals."

Simpler. Was that disgruntled woman justified in her remarks? Have we made Christmas too complex? In our compulsive search for perfection, have we perhaps lost the ability to appreciate little things? When Christmas degenerates into lavish productions, does any of it really mean anything?

In this vein, never can I forget the Christmas specials produced by one of America's most glamorous talk show hosts. The setting for her most recent one was her opulent western mansion in the Rockies. There were two stage sets: the outside one, a veritable winter wonderland, complete with snow-encrusted pine trees and a backdrop of snow-capped mountains; and the inside one, perfection personified: tens of thousands of dollars having been spent on decorations alone. That Christmas program, like those before, was a blockbuster, complete with the requisite celebrities—and children, naturally, her own. The music, secular as well as spiritual, was splendidly performed.

Later, I heard two people talking about it. One said, "I can't really tell you what was wrong with it, for it was beautiful—but still . . . it lacked something—"

The second broke in, "*I* can tell you what was wrong. It missed the whole meaning of Christmas, at least in a spiritual sense. It was almost as if I could hear her say, 'Am I not just about the most beautiful woman you've ever seen? And how about my kids—aren't they just too adorable for words! And don't you wish you could afford to live in gorgeous homes like *we* do?'"

I said to myself, "They're right. That's what I missed in that much-hyped TV special; the reason for the season. Self-adoration is a mighty poor substitute for the Babe in a manger."

So what can we do about it?

The solution is an easy one. Each of us can construct a counterforce to the media Christmas programming that each year turns out to be more secularized than the one before. How can we pull off such a revolution? Following are some ways:

Stop trying to impress people. Instead, just be yourself. Don't spend what you can ill afford, just to keep up with the neighbors.

Paradoxically, just as the ultimate prestige item (in terms of written communication) is the handwritten letter today, just so the most valued Christmas present is something that was handmade or home-cooked by the giver. In a world where most everything we receive for Christmas has been mass-produced in sweatshop environments by minimum wage (or less) workers overseas, what a serendipity it is to receive a gift created by the giver! Sadly, we've all but lost the age-old tradition of giving from the heart. We give *things*, we give *money*, but rarely do we give of ourselves. We're much more likely to bury our children in creature comforts than to give them personal time, than to give them things money cannot buy. This Christmas, let us go back to the old ways.

The greatest Christmas stories remind us that Christ and Christlike selfless giving ought to be at the core of our celebrations of Christmas. We should give anonymously as often as possible—perhaps the most difficult type of giving there is. Though Christ urged us to give "in secret," how few of us follow the divine admonition. How few of us give to those who are not able to give back. Reciprocity—getting back gifts of at least equal value—appears to be our yearly norm.

Nor should we forget deserving causes, ministries such as the Salvation Army, at Christmas. There are so many such organizations and needs that ought to be remembered. Perhaps the most powerful story on this subject is Nancy Rue's "The Red Envelope" in *Christmas in My Heart* 7.

Sacrifice is almost an obsolete word in today's money-conscious society. In fact, it's a difficult gift for wealthy parents

11

to pass on to their children. Yet, unless children learn how to give sacrificially, they are predisposed to grow up self-centered. The most memorable Christmas stories generally incorporate some form of sacrificial giving into the plot. If a child has never had to sacrifice for the good of others, that child will most likely grow up spiritually stunted.

Today, more and more, electronics are eroding Christmas family celebrations. My sister, Marji, started a new tradition in her home: it is understood that their house is an electronics-free zone. Instead of electronic games, Game Boys, TV, etc., board games enable the entire family to make memories together. After one Christmas in which electronics all but wrecked our time together, we adopted that tradition too. Children love it because above all they covet undivided time with *us*—not with mere electronic gadgetry. Indeed, one author put it this way: "children spell love 'T-I-M-E.' "

Storytelling was almost extinct in America, but appears to be coming back. There is magic in telling or reading stories to one's family at Christmas. They'll forget the gifts you give them—but they'll never forget the most deeply moving stories you share with them. Many families begin reading Christmas stories on Thanksgiving Day evening, and continue until Epiphany (or Day of the Wise Men) on January 6. That means that thirty-six days (or one-tenth of the calendar year) may be colored by the beauty of character-building stories. The more loved they are, the more they'll be requested and remembered.

Beloved Christmas films, used judiciously and sparingly, offer a change of pace. Films such as *It's a Wonderful Life* and *A Christmas Carol* are timeless classics that deserve to live on.

Music, too, ought to be an integral part of our Christmases. There is so much we can do during this season to introduce our children to great Christmas music (home-performed as well as professionally performed). Oratorios such as *Messiah* add a special dimension to each Christmas. Children are natural hams and love to participate in home musical programs, skits, and dramas. Nativity plays help them to understand Christ's birth on earth in ways abstractions fail to.

Strange as it may seem, the fondest Christmas memories generally have to do with tough times, not when gifts came in torrents. Consequently, we should do our utmost to share tough times stories with our children so that they, vicariously at least, will learn now to appreciate less rather than more.

One of the greatest gifts we can bequeath to our children is requiring them to purchase Christmas gifts with money that *they* have earned. An even greater gift is to require every member of the family to create their own gifts. Pearl Buck's great story, "Christmas Day in the Morning" (*Christmas in My Heart* 4), about a teenager whose Christmas gift to his father was getting up in the middle of the night to milk all the cows before his father got up, is especially moving.

A significantly large number of stories have to do with affluence, and how it almost invariably erodes personal relationships, especially marriages. In that respect, it may not be surprising to learn that Temple Bailey's "The Candle in the Forest" (*Christmas in My Heart* 3) is being read more and more by engaged couples or young marrieds as a template for keeping love young throughout life, in good times and in bad.

Family traditions—how much poorer Christmas would be without them. The ornaments and decorations children made in years gone by should not only be preserved, they should be used even after the children have grown. Perhaps the most

moving such story is Agnes Turnbull's "Merry Little Christmas" (*Christmas in My Heart* 5). For our own family, it would be unthinkable to skip the annual trading game (see my story "Hans and the Trading Game" [*Christmas in My Heart* 5]).

I have, as a historian of ideas, long been fascinated by the phenomenon called *fin de siècle* (last decade of a century); how each century turn results in a seismic impact on a society, how each five-hundred-year turn has a much greater ideological fruit-basket upset, and how millennial turns shake the very foundations of the world. With this in mind, I've been intently studying the first decade of our new millennium. It wouldn't at all surprise me to see it begin with a global depression on the scale of the 1930s (hopefully, shorter in length, however). But one thing appears certain, the world Americans have taken for granted is no more. For half a century, Americans have been profligate with money they did not possess, running up indebtedness they could never—short of a miracle—pay off. This gigantic house of cards has collapsed, and no one knows what will replace it or how long it will take to create a new societal template.

Which makes this particular introduction eerily prescient: proposing, at least for the 10 percent of the year we label the Christmas season, that we return to a simpler model. That we make it once again a time for families to gather together for renewal and memory-making; that once again the three generations will borrow from each other's strengths; that the wisdom of the old will be respected and its counsel respectfully heeded. That we celebrate each day, each evening, of the Advent and Christmastide. That we read a special Christmas story each evening. That we develop our God-given talents and make our Christmas gifts by hand. That we will give sac-rificially to those too poor to give back—anonymously if at all possible. That we will, with our children, take time to visit the sick, the lonely, those who are rarely visited. That we will revel in the music and dramas that so enrich this season. That we will continue in the family traditions, which make us who we are, and make new ones just as meaningful. That we will play outdoor games and board games inside, not merely stare glassy-eyed at electronic imagery. That above all, Christ will reign at the heart of all we do and say.

The result is a no-brainer: for such a Christmas, who would not travel a thousand miles just to be home—*for home is where your story begins*.

About this collection

Way back at the beginning, I made a vow to God that if ever I should feel that a given collection of *Christmas in My Heart*® stories was weaker than those that came before, I'd close the series with that collection. Instead, each year I've felt that this one could very well be the best yet. That's especially a tough order after the great *St. Nicholas* collection last year, but I'm convicted that this one, too, will stand the test of time. Of course, I never know for sure until I hear from devoted readers like you.

Though we've anthologized a number of Mabel McKee's stories in other genre collections, this is her first appearance in *Christmas in My Heart*® since "Bethany's Christmas Carol" way back in our very first collection in 1992. It is also the second appearance for three contemporary writers. They are living proof that great Christmas stories are still being written. They are Marlene J. Chase, Jean Jeffrey Gietzen, and Isobel Stewart. This is Christine Whiting Parmenter's fourth appearance—no one who has read her "David's Star of Bethlehem" (*Christmas in My Heart* 1) will ever be able to forget her. Which brings us to two writers who have carried this series on their capable shoulders: This is Temple Bailey's eighth appearance and Margaret E. Sangster Jr.'s eleventh! Though both are no longer with us, through their inimitable stories they continue to live on in our hearts. As always, we also have first timers: Idona Hill, Carolyn Abbott Stanley, Ruth Herrick Myers, Frank Bennett, Diane Rayner, Claire Jones, and Anna Sprague Packard.

So the jury's out on this collection—and won't come in until you start writing me with your reactions.

CODA

I look forward to hearing from you! Please do keep the stories, responses, and suggestions coming—and not just for Christmas stories. I am putting together collections centered on other genres as well. You may reach me by writing to:

Joe L. Wheeler, PhD
P.O. Box 1246
Conifer, CO 80433

May the Lord bless and guide the ministry of these stories in your home.

---

1. *Encyclopedia Britannica*, 15th ed., s.v. "Shakers."

The Magic of the Season

Isobel Stewart

"I would be the quietest, bestest sheep you've ever seen, Miss Martin," Rebecca assured her.

But Miss Martin had grave doubts. Doubts about the attractive new minister too. It looked like it was going to be a very mixed-up Christmas.

* * * * *

"D on't want to be a nangel," Rebecca said firmly.

"You don't want to be an angel?" Beth repeated, taken aback.

Every *other* little girl taking part in the Nativity play wanted to be an angel—if she couldn't be Mary, of course.

She looked down at the small, dark-haired girl, brows drawn together very fiercely, lower lip mutinous.

So this was why Rebecca had waited after the other children had gone.

"You know why Karen's going to be Mary, Rebecca," she said carefully. "She's older, and she has to learn to say quite a lot."

"I know Karen's going to be Mary," Rebecca replied impatiently. "I just wanted to tell you that I don't want to be a nangel."

"Why not?" Beth asked.

"I don't want to wear one of those stupid nangel suits!" Rebecca said scornfully.

In spite of herself, Beth's lips twitched, but she managed to keep her face straight.

"So what do you want to be?" she asked. "Shepherd? Or a wise man?"

Rebecca shook her head. "I want to be a sheep," she said firmly.

Beth's heart sank.

"But we already have these lovely pretend animals, the ones we use every year," she reminded the little girl.

"You know, there's the donkey and three sheep, and Mr. Johnson has even made a cow for us this year."

Rebecca's eyes, clear and blue, held Beth's unwaveringly. She didn't say anything.

"Well, I suppose we could have one more sheep," Beth said, after a moment's thought.

And then, because she had come to know Rebecca pretty well indeed in the three years she'd been teaching Sunday School and organizing the Nativity play, she said sternly, "But you'd have to be a very good sheep, Rebecca, a *quiet* sheep!"

"I would be the quietest, bestest sheep you've ever seen, Miss Martin," Rebecca assured her.

"Here's my mummy come to collect me. Can I tell her I'm going to be a sheep?"

Beth nodded, and watched the child run across the hall to join the young woman who had just come in with Rebecca's little brother in his stroller.

When they were ready to go, Rebecca zipped herself into her warm jacket and, proudly pushing the pram, waved to

Beth who waved in return and then turned to tidy the small stage where the Nativity play would be performed.

"You handled that very well, Beth," David Wilson said, coming through the doorway that led to his study.

"I'm not so sure about that," Beth replied ruefully. "I'm afraid you don't know Rebecca. She has a natural talent for creating chaos.

"Last year, she was one of the four little ones holding up letters to spell *Star*, and guess what?"

The young minister burst out laughing.

"She got all the kids round the wrong way?" he guessed rightly. "You wouldn't be the first Nativity play to have *Rats* instead of a *Star*!"

"I just don't know what she'll do as a sheep," Beth said, putting the empty crib in its storage place under the stage.

David lifted the stable door down from the stage, and put it beside the crib.

"I wanted to be through here earlier," he said, "but I'm afraid I got caught up finishing off Sunday's sermon.

"I enjoyed your last rehearsal, Beth. You're very good with the children."

"I enjoy doing the Nativity play," Beth replied, really meaning it.

"And you enjoy teaching in Sunday School, I can see that," David said.

He smiled and Beth thought again, as she had more and more in the six months he had been here, what a nice warm smile he had.

And it was a smile without any hint in it of the sadness he must feel.

No one knew any details, of course, just that there had been some personal sorrow in his life; some girl he had—what was it his housekeeper had said—loved and lost.

It was difficult to believe, Beth had sometimes thought, that this unknown girl had preferred someone else.

But perhaps she had decided she didn't want to be married to a minister.

Or perhaps—

* * * * *

"Mrs. Brown had just taken coffee through to the study for me," David interrupted her reverie. "Come and have some. It'll warm you up before you head for home."

Beth knew the study well, for she had come here for Bible class and youth groups, and later for Sunday School teachers' meetings, when old Reverend Hansen was still here.

David hadn't changed anything, and she found that reassuring.

"I'm not very tidy, I'm afraid," he said apologetically, moving a pile of books from the desk to make room for her mug of coffee.

"Neither was Reverend Hansen," Beth assured him.

"So Mrs. Brown tells me," the young minister replied. "I gather she had hoped the new minister just might be, but she's not too surprised."

They chatted about her parents then. David knew them both, for Beth's mother was secretary of the Women's Association, and her father was on the Maintenance Committee.

"I find people here very friendly," David said.

"I did have some doubts at first—following a man like John Hansen, who'd been here for all these years, and coming

from a city church to a small town.

"It's quite a challenge, for me and my congregation!"

In the six months since he had come here, Beth had always found the young minister easy to talk to and very pleasant and friendly. But this was the first time she had been alone with him.

The old minister had been a family friend as well as her minister, and she had sat here so many times sharing her hopes and troubles, in her formative years.

And she had listened, too, both here and in her own home, as the old man had talked of his own worries, especially during the years of his wife's failing health, and his concern about his grown-up children.

"Ministers are just people, like the rest of us," her father had said more than once. "Reverend or not, just people with lives to live, same as the rest of us."

And so it was very easy for her to listen now, as David, the young minister, told her about his own mother, a fiercely independent widow, and about his sister, Edna, and her two little boys, and how much he missed them.

She wondered for a moment if he would go on and tell her something about his broken romance, but instead he spoke about her job in the lawyer's office.

"You're Jim Dale's secretary, I believe," he began.

"I don't know about secretary," Beth told him honestly. "I type his letters and answer the phone."

She thought about it. "And I remind him when

it's his wife's birthday, and when it's his turn to pick his kids up after school!"

"Then you're definitely his secretary!" David repeated.

He stood up. "I could do with some exercise," he said briskly. "I'll walk you home, and you can tell me some more about the kids in Sunday School—especially Rebecca."

It was a cold, clear night, and they talked about whether they might have snow for Christmas.

It wasn't a long walk but Beth realized afterwards, with some surprise, that they seemed to find an awful lot of things to talk about—from memories of childhood Christmases, through school days and good and bad teachers, on to detective stories, which they both admitted enjoying.

"Good night, Beth," David said when they reached her home, opening the garden gate for her.

"I'll look in on your next rehearsal. I can't wait to see that small sheep in action!"

"Yes, it could be pretty entertaining!" Beth agreed with a giggle. "Good night, David."

As she closed the door, she watched his tall figure, well muffled against the cold, striding down the street.

A nice man, she thought again—*and nice of him to walk me home, on a cold night like this.*

And—a thought that rather startled her—*silly girl, whoever she is and wherever she is, to give up such a nice young man.*

Whether it was something about that thought, or some reason that she preferred not to think too much about, she was glad that this was her parents' bridge night, and she'd be in bed before they got home.

There were only the dogs and the cat to ask her why she was a little later than usual, she thought, fending off the big dog and the small one, and listening to the cat telling her a long, noisy story.

* * * * *

David did come to the next rehearsal, bringing with him the P. D. James novel he had promised to lend her.

He stayed in the background while Beth rehearsed the children, but once or twice, there was the unmistakable sound of muffled laughter from his seat in the hall.

Once was when Rebecca pushed one of the shepherds into his place so briskly that he collided with a wise man, and they both fell.

The other time was when she told Mary that she was holding Baby Jesus the wrong way.

"That's not how you hold a baby," she said scornfully. "This is how you carry him."

Expertly, she hoisted the large doll on to one skinny little hip.

"See?" she said to the bewildered Mary, over her shoulder. "This is the way we carry our Kevin. Isn't this the right way, Miss Martin?"

Beth, recovering at once, stepped forward. "I'm sure it is, Rebecca," she agreed. "But I think perhaps we won't have Baby Jesus out of the crib at all. Karen can just bend over and pat him."

The rehearsal went smoothly after that. At the end, when the children had all been collected, David helped to put the props away.

Once again, his housekeeper had brought a tray with coffee and biscuits into the comfortable, untidy study, and once again David walked home with Beth.

And, when they had said good night, Beth had the sudden and disturbing realization that there were only two more rehearsals.

* * * * *

It was halfway through the next rehearsal, when Rebecca suddenly gave a very loud and prolonged *baa*.

The other children burst out laughing.

Beth, halfway through playing "We Three Kings of Orient Are," turned from the piano.

"I thought you promised to be a quiet sheep, Rebecca," she pointed out.

Rebecca's blue eyes were pools of innocence.

"I didn't mean to do that, Miss Martin," she explained. "But I was being such a real sheep, that the noise just sort of came out."

"Just see that it doesn't come out again, then," Beth told her.

"But if I don't make any sheep noises, people won't know there's a real sheep with the pretend ones," Rebecca pointed out.

"Oh, I think they'll know, all right," Beth assured her. "They'll see that—that one sheep is different.

"And that reminds me, Rebecca, if you wriggle as much as that, your sheepskin will fall off."

Beth's mother's small bedside rug was tied around Rebecca, as firmly as possible while still allowing her to breathe, but it was under severe strain.

"I'll try," Rebecca said in a small, contrite voice. "But my tummy feels tickly inside with excitement and then I can't help wriggling."

"Wriggles and baas," Beth said ruefully to David as they walked away from the hall later.

"I just have the strangest feeling that I'm going to be sorry I said Rebecca could be a sheep!"

* * * * *

Rather to her surprise, the dress rehearsal went well, although Beth couldn't help a strong feeling of disappointment that David wasn't there.

She did remind herself, severely, that on this Christmas Eve morning he had so much to do, that she shouldn't even have thought he would have time to come.

And it wasn't as if she really needed help to set everything out because the older children were only too glad to help.

Even Rebecca was quiet and cooperative, tucking the blanket around Baby Jesus in his crib, kneeling beside the other animals in silence.

The dress rehearsal had been held in the church, instead of in the hall, because the play was to form part of the morning service on Christmas Day.

When the children had gone, Beth went back through to the hall to finish decorating the Christmas tree, to be ready for the special tea that would follow the service tomorrow.

Sandra Craig, one of the other Sunday School teachers, was to have helped her to do this, but she had phoned that morning to say she had a dreadful toothache and was going to the dentist.

Beth didn't mind. She always enjoyed decorating the tree, and she hummed her way through her favorite Christmas carols as she worked.

She was halfway through "Once in Royal David's City," when the hall door opened, and David came in.

"Hi," he said, coming across to her. "I'm glad you're still here—I've been rushing around trying to find someone to play the organ tomorrow. Jane Warden has the flu.

"I've managed to persuade St. Thomas's organist to come here right after their service, which is early. I was afraid I'd missed you. How did the dress rehearsal go?"

"Surprisingly well," Beth told him. "Everything's ready. I just need to finish the tree. This afternoon, my mother and her team will be here to get the trestle tables ready."

"I'll help you," David said.

He took two glass baubles carefully from her. "You're not tall enough to reach up with these, anyway."

It was a case of teamwork after that, with Beth handing David the decorations that had to be put high up on the tree.

"Looks nice, doesn't it?" he said with satisfaction, inspecting the star at the top.

"I'm glad I've been in on this. I was thinking just yesterday how much I miss decorating the tree at home.

"My mother's having Edna's little boys for the day. They'll be helping."

He smiled and shook his head. "I phoned her last night and she said they'd miss me, and I said I'd miss them.

"She hates to think of me on my own on Christmas Day, although she knows Mrs. Brown will leave me a nice meal."

Beth hesitated. If it wasn't for the thought of that un-known girl, she would have asked him to join her family.

Mum and Dad would be delighted, she knew that, and so would Gran, Ted, Sylvia, and the children.

But, but perhaps he'd rather be on his own, with his memories.

"I suppose mothers always worry about their children," David said then, and she thought she must have imagined the faint regret in his eyes, because now he was smiling.

"Oh, they do," she agreed fervently. "My mother must be just about the worst. She worries that I'll catch cold in winter, and that I'll get too many freckles in summer.

"And she worries because I'm twenty-nine and not married!"

They were both kneeling now, putting the tiny glass lanterns onto the lowest branches.

"So there isn't anyone special in your life, Beth?" David asked casually. "I must admit that surprises me."

Beth shrugged. "Just never met the right person," she said truthfully.

The young minister hesitated, but only for a moment. "And your mother worries because you're not married?" he asked.

His hand brushed against hers, as he adjusted a small lantern. "So does mine."

"But—" Beth stopped.

"But what?" David asked.

Beth swallowed. "She—she must have been very sad for you when your—your romance broke up," she said with difficulty.

David was silent for so long that she wished she hadn't said it.

And then, to her surprise, she saw that he was blushing.

"Actually," he said, "I've been wanting to talk to you about that. To explain."

"Oh, you don't have to do that," Beth told him hurriedly. "There's no need."

She was pretty sure that she was blushing now as well. She hoped, fervently, that he hadn't thought that she was—

"But I *do* need to explain," David said with conviction, interrupting her thoughts.

He sat back on his heels, and Beth did the same. "You see, Beth, there wasn't any romance, or any breakup."

She looked at him, not understanding.

David sighed. "I'm not very proud of myself," he said after a moment.

"But, when Mrs. Brown began asking me about girlfriends and saying how difficult it must be for a minister without a wife, I . . . kind of panicked."

"I didn't exactly say, but somehow she got the impression that I had—"

"Loved and lost?" Beth broke in helpfully.

There was a very strange feeling somewhere inside her, around where her heart was.

"It was a kind of protection," David said. "I've been wanting you to know that I didn't really mean to deceive anyone."

Beth couldn't think what to say to that, so she said nothing. But the strange, warm feeling was growing, a sort of bubble of happiness.

Not only because of what David had said, but because of the way he was looking at her.

"And your mother worries about you too?" he asked.

And she realized that he hadn't taken the tinsel she was handing him. Instead, his hands were holding hers, with the tinsel between them.

She nodded. "I told her once that maybe I needed a prince on a white charger, coming right to the front door," she said.

"And Mum said, if that happened, I'd probably keep the white charger, and send the prince away!"

"You like white chargers?" David asked gravely.

"I like all animals," Beth said, not quite steadily.

* * * * *

She wasn't sure, afterwards, which of them moved forward first.

But his lips were on hers, and she couldn't believe it was really happening.

They both heard the sound at the same time—a baby crying—through the open door that led to the church.

Beth and David scrambled to their feet and reached the door at the same time.

The cry came again.

And it came from the crib.

A small fist appeared—*a real fist,* Beth thought, unbelieving, *not a doll's.*

The baby looked up at them, and his tears stopped as if by magic.

He smiled and held out his arms, some of the straw from the crib clutched in one fat little hand.

Beth's thoughts of abandoned orphan babies left in a place of safety, stopped whirling.

"It's Rebecca's baby brother, Kevin!"

There was no doubt in either of their minds that if Rebecca's baby brother was here in the crib, Rebecca must know something about it.

The baby in the crib decided that enough was enough.

Since the smiles hadn't worked, he switched back to crying again.

As he drew in his breath for another loud yell, Beth scooped him up in her arms.

"That's better, isn't it, Kevin?" she asked him.

And miraculously it was. The tears and the yells stopped as if by magic and the wide, toothless smile was there again.

Beth had had plenty of experience with family babies and little Kevin obviously felt confident in her arms.

"What now?" David asked. "I know Rebecca lives just down the street. Should we take him home?"

"We wait for Rebecca to come back," Beth told him.

They didn't have to wait long.

* * * * *

A small figure appeared at the door of the church, mittened hands firmly on the handle of the pram.

Halfway down the aisle, Rebecca stopped. "Oh," she said in a small voice.

Beth opened her mouth, but David's hand on her arm stopped her from saying anything.

"Like to tell us what's going on, Rebecca?" he asked gently.

Rebecca took a deep breath. "I thought Baby Jesus must get awful fed up just lying there in the crib, so I took him for a walk.

"There wasn't enough room for Kevin, too, so I left him in the crib.

"Anyway," she said quickly, "it looked kind of funny with no baby in it. But I did think I'd get Baby Jesus back before anyone saw."

She looked from the minister to her Sunday School teacher, and what she saw in their faces brought a slow thank-goodness-you're-not-going-to-be-angry smile to her small, freckled face.

"I'd better take Kevin home now," she said.

Carefully, like a little mother, she put the Baby Jesus back in the crib, arranged the straw comfortably, and then wrapped the blanket around him.

"See you tomorrow, Baby Jesus," she whispered.

Then, with her small brother securely strapped in his stroller, she looked up at David and Beth.

"Thanks for looking after Kevin," she said. "And you don't need to worry, Miss Martin. I'll be a really quiet sheep tomorrow and I won't do a thing—even if Tommy Harper forgets when he has to give his present to Baby Jesus.

"An' I won't worry if the shepherds don't stand like you told them to. An' I won't wriggle!"

She walked demurely up the aisle again, but, at the door, she turned.

"Don't you feel wriggly, too, 'cause it's Christmas tomorrow?" she asked wonderingly.

David's hand clasped Beth's.

"I suppose we do feel a bit wriggly, Rebecca," he agreed.

They watched the small figure turn at the door, and disappear.

David looked down at Beth. "Maybe this is the first of our own special memories of Christmas, Beth."

"Maybe it is," Beth agreed, not quite steadily.

"We'd better finish the tree," he said, and he smiled. "Before the ladies get busy with their trestle tables!"

They went through to the hall, and he was still holding her hand.

I'll ask him to have Christmas dinner with us, Beth decided—*that will be another special memory for us.*

As she handed David the box with the fairy lights, she was all at once very sure that there would be so many memories, from now on, for the two of them.

Isobel Stewart has written more than fifty novels and hundreds of short stories, many of them translated into other languages. For a number of years, she wrote a weekly newspaper column for a newspaper in Windhoek, Namibia, and has also broadcasted frequently on radio in South Africa. Today she lives and writes from Helderberg Village in Somerset West, South Africa.

Oren's Christmas Present

Idona Hill

Twelve whole dollars for Christmas—all to spend on anything he wanted! It just seemed too good to be true.

But on the way to town to place his order, something absolutely unforeseen happened.

* * * * *

With a catalog hanging over one knee and a writing pad on the other, Oren Hillstead, aged twelve, made out his first order. The mail the day before had brought him twelve dollars as Christmas money from his liberal Uncle Jim, to be spent at his own choosing. It was the first money of so large an amount that Oren had ever possessed all by himself. He had been a Christmas present to his parents twelve years before, and now Uncle Jim had sent him a dollar for each year. It was a fortune to him, and he felt joyful that he could have the things he had wanted so long. The order read,

6K210½	Stevens' Little Scout Rifle, .22-caliber	$5.20
6L5211	New Victor Giant Trap no. 1	
	(for mink and muskrat), 1 dozen	$2.63
6K5085	Best Grade Hockey Skates	$2.55
	Total..............$10.38	

He finished writing just as Mother took the warm plates from the oven and announced, "Breakfast is ready."

"Say, Father," he asked, "may I walk over to Boxelder today and send this order off? I want it to go right way, and it'll go quicker from there than it will from Mason."

"What's the rush, Son? The snow is deep. You know it's pretty snappy outside, and we'll be going down to Mason tomorrow. Besides, I have to use the team this morning, and if you go to Boxelder you will have to walk."

"I don't care about the walk. I want to get these things as soon as I can, and you know Mason hasn't any railroad, and the order won't get on the train before Thursday if I mail it at Mason."

"Well, climb the snowbanks if you want to. I suppose it will be good exercise," his father consented.

With fur-lined cap, heavy mackinaw, and overshoes, Oren ventured out upon the eight miles of unbroken road to Boxelder. The snow in the road proved deep and hard to climb through, and after two or three miles of hard wading, he decided to try a crosscut through the fields.

This worked better for a time, and he trudged along, dreaming of the fun he would have with his long-desired possessions. Suddenly coming over the top of a hill, he found himself entering a barnyard with a house a few rods beyond. The place appeared neglected, and the neighing of horses and the bellowing of a cow caused Oren to look into the barn. He found mangers empty of feed, and the animals gaunt from hunger and thirst.

"I'll just stop at the house and ask the way to Boxelder, and maybe I can find out what's the matter," Oren decided.

A little child answered his knock and invited him to come in.

"I want to see your papa," Oren said.

"Papa and Mama are sick," the child answered, crying. "I guess they've got the flu, and we haven't any money or anything to eat, and we're all hungry." Two other little children soon appeared, begging him to come in and see their papa and mama.

"It is a great blessing that someone has come," the father spoke. "If you can't help us much, perhaps you can call someone."

"I'll do the best I can. What shall I do first?"

"If you can find any fuel, please build a fire for the children, and feed and water the animals in the barn," the father requested.

A few sticks of wood were found and a fire was built. The famished animals were cared for, and Oren tried to get some milk from the cow for the little ones. When this was done, he returned to the house with only enough milk for the baby. The other children cried for food, and Oren asked what he could do for them.

"We haven't a thing in the house to eat, and we can't get a cent's credit at the store until we pay what we owe. I don't know what we can do. If we could only borrow enough money to get through this trouble, I would pay it back as soon as I can get to work. It's hard to hear the children cry for something to eat."

For an instant the gun, the traps, and the skates loomed big before the boy's eyes, and

then the cry of the smallest child, "Daddy, hungry!" resolved the boy to make the biggest sacrifice he had ever made.

"Well, I'll see what I can do for you," Oren answered, and went out to the barn. Hitching the strongest-looking horse to a wagon, he drove to Boxelder.

"If I only knew what I ought to buy. I'll ask somebody in the store," he decided.

The purchase was made as soon as possible. With five dollars, he bought one bushel of potatoes, one package of oatmeal, one peck of beans, two pounds of butter, three loaves of bread, one dozen eggs, three quarts of milk, and one pound of sugar. He also bought a few supplies for the sick, at the advice of the druggist. With the seven dollars remaining, he bought coal.

Suppose I should have got some flour, he thought. *But they're too hungry to wait for bread to be baked, and there is no one there to bake it, anyway. Tomorrow Mother can come over, maybe, and bring a little flour and bake some bread. I guess I have done about all I can.* Then he drove back to the farmhouse.

Unloading the things, Oren began to realize that it would be his job to get supper for the family. It was a new task to him, but he went at it like a veteran, and felt himself the happiest boy in the world when the hungry little ones gathered around the table.

After supplying the needs of the father and mother as best he could, he set out on the long walk home, stopping at the first house to ask someone to stay with the family that night.

"Well, Son," his father said, as he threw off his cap and mackinaw, "so you got that important order off today, did you?"

"What order?" Oren really had forgotten.

"Why, your gun, of course. I didn't think you would forget that for a minute."

"Oh! I guess I was thinking about something else," Oren answered. "Fact is," he explained, "I found a starving family."

"*Starving!*" repeated Mother, as she looked up from her mending.

Oren detested explanations, so with as few words as possible he told of the plight of the family that lived on the way to Boxelder. Mother was immediately full of plans. Mother always seemed to have good ones stored away for just such times of need. She and Oren undertook to see the little family through their siege of illness, and what they undertook was usually done. At any rate, comfort, warmth, and care reigned in the place of cold and hunger for the invalids just over the hill.

* * * * *

Three weeks later, his father again said, "Son, it seems strange your things don't come. It's three weeks now since you sent the order, and you haven't even heard from it. It would have come just as quick from Mason, and you wouldn't have had that long walk. Are you sure you wrote 'Chicago' on the envelope?"

"Father, that order didn't go to Chicago. I sent it to another place."

"It would have had time to come from Capetown before this," his father teased.

Oren looked seriously into his father's face. "Father," he said, "I sent it to the New Jerusalem."

Idona Hill wrote around the turn of in the twentieth century.

So This Is Christmas!

Temple Bailey

The lovely nurse with hair like burnished flame wanted more than the young doctor could offer her. Much much more! And told him so. And then she left. Left for the great mansion of her dreams.

But when she got there, beneath the veneer was emptiness, beneath the jollity was something sinister. All around her swirled the Christmas of her dreams. Only trouble was— Christ was nowhere to be found.

* * * * *

If you will eat your soup, I will tell you a story," said the redheaded nurse.

"What kind of soup?"

"Chicken."

"Chicken shadow? Or the real thing?"

"Real. One of the Red Cross women brought it. It has noodles in it." The redheaded nurse fairly sparkled with her knowledge of its deliciousness.

The man sitting on the edge of the bed could not see the sparkle. He was going blind, and the redheaded nurse was simply a blurred shadow against the shine of the lamp beyond.

"I'm not hungry," he said.

"Please. I can't stay if you don't. And I've so much to tell you."

"Tell it anyhow."

"If you'll taste one spoonful."

"Oh, well . . ."

"It's about myself."

He began to be interested. "What's happened?"

"I have an invitation, if you please. And a dress with it. An old school friend of mine has hunted me up and has asked me to a Christmas ball at her house. And her mother is my godmother and has given me the things to wear—the loveliest green gown for the party, with silver lace on it. And silver slippers. I am to stay from the evening before Christmas, which is tonight, until the morning after."

He had been trying to eat the soup, finding his lips carefully with the spoon. Letting the noodles go because one *couldn't*. It was bad enough if one had eyes.

He laid the spoon down. "That means, of course, you'll not be here on Christmas Day."

"I can't be. I'm sorry. But this is such a treat . . . And you'll hardly know that I'm gone. I am planning everything so that you boys will have your tree and get your presents."

"Presents . . ." There was weary scorn in his voice. He wanted to say, *What can they give me? I'm going blind . . . I'm going blind . . . I'm going blind!* But of course he couldn't say it. It wouldn't be sporting. None of the boys whined. He wanted the redheaded nurse to go away. He wanted to pull the bed covers over his head. He wanted to cry like a baby.

Yet he wanted her, too, to stay, so that he might be held

back for a moment from that awful blackness, which engulfed him when he was alone.

She always talked about pleasant commonplaces in such a pretty way. She had told him a lot about herself. That her mother had died, and that her father had married again, and had failed in business, and she had taken nurse's training so that there might be money enough to go round.

She began now to describe the tree that she had helped to trim. "There's to be one in each ward. I think ours is the nicest. It has an angel on top and silver stars and pale blue lights. It gives it a sort of mystical look. Different."

He knew why she was describing it thus minutely. Lending him her eyes. So that he might tomorrow morning see it with an inner vision.

She went on, "I'm dying to tell you about your present."

Some of the blackness fell from him. "What is it?"

"No . . . I mustn't spoil it. But I'll tell you about some of the others." She whispered, so that the boys in the surrounding beds would be none the wiser. Her voice was like that of an eager child. And while she talked she fed him his soup. Usually he hated that. It seemed to emphasize his helplessness. But she did it so deftly that he was hardly conscious of eating it, noodles and all, to the very bottom of the bowl.

She had to leave him then. "I'm going to say 'Good night' and 'Goodbye' together. I won't try to wish you 'A merry Christmas,' Pinkney. It can't be that. But I shall wish you a brave one."

"Wishing won't make me brave. I'm a coward. I don't want to have to . . . go on . . ."

Whining! That was it! But he didn't care!

Yet her handclasp heartened him, and when she had gone,

he got out some pricked cards she had given him and began a game of solitaire.

The redheaded nurse passing down the ward found other men in other beds. A cheerful lot if one looked only on the surface. A sporting lot. Most of them knew there wasn't much ahead for them. They all liked the nurse. She was a laughter-loving little thing, and spent herself in service for them. She was pretty, too, and young, but with no nonsense about her. They liked her name, which was Patricia Gayworthy. They felt that it suited her. Some of them called her "Miss Pat" and some of them called her "Miss Gay," but either way they liked it.

As she went among them tonight, she was aware of a certain lowness of mind in all of them. She tried to think of pleasant things to say to brighten them up a bit. But it wasn't easy. She knew that what they wanted on Christmas Eve was not platitudes but hearthstones.

Going out, she met the doctor in charge of the ward. His name was Grant, and he had served overseas. He was young, but not as young as the redheaded nurse. He had seen hard service on the other side and had been a bit worn down by it. He was working too hard, and the only light in his day was the redheaded nurse. He was in love with her. He was not sure that she knew it. He had planned to tell her on Christmas Day.

And now she was saying, "I'm going to be very grand and gorgeous. I'm going away tonight. To a house party. I won't be back until day after tomorrow."

"Oh, but look here, you can't."

"Why not?"

"Because we can't spare you."

"Who is 'we'?"

"Everybody. What kind of Christmas will the boys have without you?"

"I'm not so important. And anyhow, I want some fun myself. I'm not a saint or a Sister of Charity. I'm human. I've got to see some happy people. Here there's just Pinkney's eyes," there were tears in her own, "and Bruelle . . . dying . . ."

"I know." Then after a silence, "When do you leave?"

"I am going over now to the nurses' quarters to change. My bags are packed. My hostess is sending her chauffeur for me! They dine at eight, and after that there's the dance and a tree."

"And you won't be back tomorrow?"

"Not till the day after."

"Hmm . . . Well, I call it rather shabby of you."

"Don't you want me to be happy?"

"Of course. But I want to be happy too."

She had a wisp of a smile for his paraphrase of the popular song. "You'd better run away."

"I can't."

"Why not?"

"The other fellows want to eat Christmas dinner with their families. I'm the only bachelor in the bunch."

They were walking now towards the nurses' quarters. "You ought to have a house of your own," she told him with fine unconsciousness.

"I want it," he said, "with you in it."

She gasped, "But how could I?"

"I am asking you to marry me. I intended to do it tomorrow. But you are going away."

Recovering from the first shock, she said, "Of course I couldn't."

"Why not?"

"Because I like you a lot. But not that way."

"What way?"

The wind blowing a great blast, almost swept her from her feet. He anchored her with a firm grip on her arm. "What way?" he asked again.

She considered it for a moment as he stood with his body shielding her. The lights of the hospital twinkled in rows to the right of them, the lights of the nurses' quarters twinkled in rows to the left of them. Between was a stretch of snowy ground, overhead was a fleecy sky, with the moon racing.

"Well, I'm not in love with you . . ." was her final explanation.

"How do you know?"

"If I loved you, I'd want to marry you. And I don't."

His grip on her arm hurt her. "Do you think I am going to let it go at that? Why don't you want to marry me?"

"Because I am a mercenary little beast. Once upon a time my father had money. And I liked it. And I'd like to have it again. I want a husband who can give me things. I want a husband like my friend has where I am going to the party. I want a town house and a country house, and motorcars and a yacht. And lovely clothes. And fur coats. And I shouldn't be happy without them."

She thought she was saying dreadful things. Things that would make him fall out of love with her. But instead, he laughed. "You don't know your own mind and heart. You were happier tonight feeding Pinkney his soup than you'd be with a thousand motorcars."

"Oh, did you see us?"

"Yes. They all adore you. They'll have a rotten Christmas without you."

"You men are all alike. Trying to make me stay. Pinkney did. But I'm not going to think about you. I'm going to think about myself."

She began to walk on, outwardly unconcerned, but inwardly acutely aware of his nearness, as he still shielded her from the wind. "You mustn't think I don't appreciate you," she said, after they had gone a little way in silence, "and the wonderfulness of your caring for me. You are fine and good, and a darling with the boys. It's just that I'm a selfish little beast."

"You're not that. And this isn't the end of things. It's the beginning." He caught up her hands and kissed them. They had reached the nurses' quarters, and he stood, still holding her hands, while she gave him some last instructions about the boys.

"I bought a music box for Pinkney. A fine little Swiss one—and it plays such gay little tunes. I wanted something for his ears—everything else seemed to be for his eyes."

"The specialist who examined Pinkney is to telephone tonight what he thinks."

"You mean that there may be—hope?"

"I'm afraid not—"

"Oh—he's so patient. Poor fellow."

She tried to withdraw her hands, and he kissed them. Then he let her go. She ran up the steps, and called down from the top, "A merry Christmas!"

He lifted his cap and the light shone on the gray of his hair. She had a little lump in her throat. He was like Pinkney. He needed her. Some of the gray had come from those dreadful experiences overseas.

But then, she couldn't always be thinking about other people. And she wasn't going to marry just because a man's gray hair hurt her to think about. She was going to put on the green dress and the silver slippers and dance until daylight!

It was seven o'clock when Patricia reached her destination. The house was huge, and high iron gates were swung wide for the motorcars to sweep through, and there was a butler at the front door, and a footman on the stairs, and a maid in your room to help you dress.

But before the maid could lift a finger, the redheaded nurse had to be embraced by her friend Barbara, who was called Babs for short, and who had been at school Patricia's best beloved. And Babs was more beautiful than ever, and had a baby.

"To *think*," she emphasized, "that you've never seen him, and he's five years old. And you've never seen my husband. We were so long abroad. Nick is mad about it."

"And you?"

"I'm not sure. Things are different over there. More sophisticated."

Babs was different. Lighted with a new brilliance. Patricia was not sure she liked it. The old Babs had seemed so utterly herself. This new Babs seemed to shine with a hardness like diamonds. "She used to be—wax candles," Patricia remembered.

They went to the nursery, and there was Babs's baby, asleep in a quaint mahogany bed, with carved angels at the four corners. At the foot of the bed hung a stocking, tied up with red ribbon and a bit of holly. A middle-aged woman, spick and span in white linen, was reading a book by a shaded lamp. She rose as they entered.

"I see that you've hung up his stocking, Nonny," Babs said.

"He hung it up himself, dear lamb, like the one in his storybook."

Patricia wondered why Babs had not been there to help him hang the stocking. She felt that if the child had been her own, she would have begrudged every moment of mirth that she did not share.

"He's such a handsome laddie," his mother was saying. "Good looking like Nick. Only Nick's hair is dark."

Patricia said, "How wonderful to have a son."

"Oh, well, of course. But sometimes it isn't wonderful. Not when Nick wants me to do things, and there's Toodles to think of. Nick doesn't like it to have me tied."

Patricia reflected that Nick, too, might like to be tied to a son like Toodles. But she didn't ask questions. And Babs said, "Pat, darling, we must run and dress—people will be coming before we know it."

Well, the maid to whom Babs entrusted her friend, massaged her and curled her and powdered her, and touched up her brows and lashes, and deepened the roses of her cheeks, and when at last the green dress was slipped over her head, and her feet were shod in the silver slippers, Patricia looked in the glass and knew she was a raving beauty!

When she went downstairs, all the men crowded about her, and at last, Babs brought her husband, who had missed a train from New York, and hardly had time to get into his dinner clothes.

And Babs's husband said to Babs's friend, "With that red hair of yours, you ought to conquer the world. All the famous beauties had red hair. Think about it, and tell me when I dance with you, if it isn't true."

He said it in an exciting way, as if what you would tell him when you danced with him would mean a great deal, and he would be up on his toes to know. He was handsome and distinguished, and it seemed wonderful that Babs should have such a husband—little Babs who had been at school with her—as it had seemed wonderful that she should have a baby.

At dinner, the two young men who sat on each side of Patricia were great fun. They flattered her a lot, and asked for all her dances, and drank quarts of champagne, and tried to get Patricia to drink it, but she told them, "Why should I? And you'd be better off without it."

They laughed at that, and one of them said, "You mustn't have such an unholy conscience. And where did you learn to listen with your eyes?"

She had learned it at the hospital, when the boys talked to her, and she had had to seem attentive or hurt their feelings. But she didn't tell this to the two young men. She wondered if they knew she was a nurse? And would it make a difference if they did?

After dinner she had a grand and glorious time. She danced and danced and danced. There didn't seem to be any end to it, and she didn't want it to end. The music was marvelous, the floor perfect, the ballroom decorations heavenly. She didn't have adjectives enough to describe it all.

Towards midnight the fun grew wild and wilder, and at last,

the two young men who sat beside her at dinner, and whom everybody called Trux and Benny, came up and said,

"Let's duck this."

"And get another girl and look at the stars."

They said it just that way, together. And Patricia surveyed them with the cool glance she reserved for derelicts at the hospital. "You're drunk," she said, "and what you need is bed and Bromo-Seltzer."

They roared at that, and said she was "ripping," and that they were going to carry her off. And the one whose name was Trux said, "You've never seen as many stars as I shall show you."

And the other, whose name was Benny, said, "Don't you believe him. He knows only one star, and that is Venus!"

Well, Babs's husband rescued her, and sent the roaring young men away. He had a dance with Patricia, he told them; which wasn't true, because she really had it with Trux. But Trux couldn't think of anything but the stars. "If you've never seen them from a Rolls-Royce," he said, "you've missed something."

"I've seen them from a Ford," was Patricia's parting shot, "and taking it all in all, perhaps it's safer."

Babs's husband danced delightfully. It was the third dance Patricia had had with him, and each time he had talked about red hair, and the wonderful women in history. "Helen and Cleopatra and the rest."

And Pat had asked him, "Were they all redheaded?"

And he had answered, "Well, at least they all had redheaded temperaments."

And now with the third dance, he was again at it. "You have temperament," he said. "Babs hasn't. Strange thing. How different you are."

Somehow the way he put it made it seem uncomplimentary to Babs. To Babs who had been the queen bee of the hive at school! To Babs who had outdistanced all of the others in her list of lovely perfections!

Patricia tried to tell him something of this, "Babs was our fairy princess in the old days."

"Fairy princesses are not always—human." Again that subtle note of disparagement. Patricia ignored it. "It seems wonderful to think that Babs is really married."

"Wonderful? Don't all pretty women marry?"

"Perhaps. But still—it's wonderful."

He looked down at her, laughing. "Why aren't you married if you think that way about it?"

"I've got to wait."

"For what?"

"Love."

"You won't have to wait long if men have their way."

"It must not be their way. But mine."

"I see. But why be so serious about it?"

"Because it's a life matter."

"Not at all. You've got the wrong slant on it. Babs and I look at it more sensibly. Neither of us thinks of marriage as a sacrament. If we should be lucky enough to go on loving each other, we'll stick it. If not, we'll be off with it. We both believe that if a man or a woman feels tied by matrimony, then it should end automatically."

Patricia flamed, "That's a horrid philosophy, I think."

"Why?"

"Oh, what would love be worth if it were so—unstable?"

He laughed again. "You are like Babs when I first met her. Old-fashioned."

Old-fashioned! Her beautiful dreaming Babs!

"I could teach you," he went on, his laughing eyes noting the flames in her own, "a glorious freedom—"

Babs came up at that moment, providentially, to ask her husband about the tree. Would he see that everything was ready? The clocks were striking twelve. While she talked she hung on his arm. It was easy to see that she adored him. And he didn't believe in constancy! He didn't believe in dreams of youth, or in aspirations, or hopes! He didn't believe in anything!

It was a most amazing tree. It hadn't anything to do with Christ and the star. It hadn't even anything to do with Santa Claus and little children. It was strange and fantastic like something out of *The Arabian Nights*. It was a great round ball of clipped yew, and hung on it were dozens and dozens of golden oranges, and each orange was a box, and in each box was a tiny gift. Coming from the top of the tree, that was crowned by a golden cupid, were floating streamers of silk, and at the end of the streamers were gold and silver balloons that floated like bubbles in the air, and the guests were given golden bows and arrows, and shot at the balloons, and for every balloon that was shot, one got a golden orange.

Patricia shot three balloons and got three oranges, and in one of them was a small vanity box, and in another a small gold pencil, and in the third, a small vial of rose perfume.

The perfume made her think of Pinkney. She had often brought him a rose, because of the fragrance. And he had said to her, "You should have seen the roses in my mother's garden."

With thoughts of Pinkney came a vision of the long room at the hospital as it would be tonight—the cold moonlight in pools on the polished floor, some of the boys asleep, others awake in their narrow beds. There would be pain there, and heartache, and fear of what was ahead. Yet there would be, too, fortitude.

And in the morning, waking to dreariness and a yearning for home, they would try to carry on.

And she would not be there to help!

With that vision upon her, she was blind at the moment to everything about her. Gone was the great ballroom crowded with dancers—the gowns of the women lighting it with superb color, rose and jade and sapphire; the tree flaunting golden streamers, the music, booming, whining, moaning—drums, saxophones, syncopation. But for Patricia there was only that long room with its cold moonlight, and the need it had of her.

She tried to tell herself that it was silly to let her mind dwell on it. That to Pinkney and Bruelle and all the rest of them her coming and going was not important. That she might as well stay and have her good time, and return home refreshed and rested. Then suddenly she knew she wasn't having a good time. She was missing something that should have been there. All about her people were shouting, "A merry Christmas." But it didn't seem to her that any of them was merry. Their voices grew louder, the fun grew fast and furious; but of real mirth, of simple satisfying happiness, she could see no sign.

The climax came when, the guests having tired of the bows and arrows, the beat of a tom-tom was heard above the clamor of voices, and through the great archway that spanned the entrance to the ballroom streamed a wild procession. Jesters were there, and slaves bearing gifts, and pages holding steaming bowls aloft, and houris dancing; and, mounted on a barrel, the Spirit of Christmas, as fat as Falstaff, and carrying a ladle.

Well, there is this to be said for Patricia, she was neither a prig nor a prude. She knew there was no harm in having fun on Christmas Eve if one wanted it. But as for herself, she didn't want it if she had to have it with those two young men who had had more than enough champagne, or with Babs's husband who wanted to teach her a glorious freedom, or with all those flushed women who seemed to have forgotten that because of a great mother, this night of all others should have been spent in their homes.

She fled to the top of the stairs and stood looking down. The men who had brought the gifts had laid them before the Falstaffian saint, who, still mounted on his barrel, beat time with his ladle to the tom-toms. And those dressed as slaves began to weave back and forth in a fantastic dance, and the houris waved their veils and jingled their bracelets, and coiled themselves like glittering snakes.

As the beat of the tom-toms grew faster, they began to sound an accompaniment to the words that echoed in Patricia's brain: "So this is Christmas . . . *so this is Christmas* . . . SO THIS IS CHRISTMAS!" said the tom-toms. But nobody heard but the girl on the stairs!

The young man called Trux looked up and saw her. He waved to her, made his way through the crowd, and began climbing the stairs. When he stumbled on the first landing, Patricia took to her heels, rushed up the remaining steps, ran down the dim hall, found her door, slammed it behind her, locked it, and leaned against it breathless.

She told herself afterwards, scornfully, that her nerves

were on edge. She had never been afraid at the hospital. Not even when the big blond Swede in the psychiatric ward had tried to brain her with a chair. She had quieted him without help, and had only been a little shaky afterwards. But tonight there was something—she couldn't quite define it—something sinister in the air. Something malevolent. Something corrupting. She had expected it would be different—fine and exquisite, a part of the old Babs, and of the dreams they had shared together. There had been nothing fine about it. She wondered if it was because against Babs's sincerity had been set the sophistication of her husband. He was, perhaps, the stronger, and Babs, loving him, had been submerged.

How dreadful to be submerged like that in another's personality! Yet if Babs's husband had been like—oh, why not say it?—like Doctor Jimmie Grant, she would not have been submerged, she would not have been carried along by a strength, which would fail her, she would have been borne up by a faith which would never falter, she would have had dreams to match her own.

Patricia had never called the doctor in charge by his first name, but now in her thoughts she spoke of him as "Jimmie." She was glad that it wasn't any more pretentious than that, just simple and boyish, belonging to him. His whole name, James Jasper Grant, had a steady ring to it, like his steady voice when he spoke to Pinkney or to poor Bruelle. She wondered what he was doing. Asleep, perhaps. Or perhaps called out of bed by poor Bruelle. She knew the comfort he would be to that passing soul. He was more than a doctor. He was a priest.

Since she was no longer frightened, she opened her door and went into the hall. At one end of it was a great window,

which looked over the hills, and reached from the ceiling to the floor. Patricia walked towards it, and stood gazing out at the stars. The night was still, and the snow lay white over the garden. Patricia thought of the hospital and the lights shining. She thought of Jimmie Grant shielding her from the wind.

She was startled by hearing a little voice at her side, "I want my Nonny."

It was Babs's baby. Adorable in pink pajamas, with sleep still in his eyes, his mop of curls standing up like a crown.

She bent down to him, "Nonny will be here presently. Will I do, until she comes? I'm a Nonny, too, you know."

"Do you take care of little boys?"

"I take care of big men. Sick ones."

He cocked his head, "Would you rather take care of little boys?"

"I would tonight. Shall we run back to bed? And I'll sit with you till your Nonny comes."

His hand was tucked in hers confidingly. "Will you tell me a story?"

"Yes. If you'll shut your eyes."

When they reached his room, the stocking still hung limp from its red ribbon.

"Santa Claus didn't come yet," Toodles confided as he climbed into bed.

"He'll come after you go to sleep."

When his head was on the pillow and the covers up to his chin, he said, "Tell me a story."

"What about?"

"Oh—Donner and Blitzen."

"I know a better one."

"What about?"

"Jesus in the manger."

"Who was Jesus-in-the-manger?"

Was this Babs's child? It seemed to Patricia incredible! Babs who had always said her prayers at school. Whose faith had seemed so steadfast.

With Toodles's hand in hers, she told him the lovely story. He listened entranced. "If Mary came here," he said, all shining with the thought of it, "and there wasn't any room, I'd sleep on the floor and give the little Baby my bed. I'd let the darling little Baby sleep in my bed." Babs's child? Or his father's?

When Toodles finally slept, Patricia still sat beside him. The nurse, coming in, asked, "Oh, did he wake?"

"Yes. And he was sweet. Nurse, he said if Mary had come here, and there had been no place to lay the Baby, he would have given up his bed."

"Oh, if they knew you had talked such things to him they wouldn't like it. They won't let me. His father doesn't want him to be narrow-minded. It almost breaks my heart."

"I didn't know. I'm glad I didn't. His mother wasn't like that!"

The redheaded nurse went back to her room, and to bed. It was a beautiful bed, and it had four pillows. She curled up and fell fast asleep. And the droning of the saxophone intruded on her dreams.

She was awakened by someone coming into her room and speaking her name, "Pats, darling."

Patricia sat up. "I've been asleep," she said superfluously.

"What on earth made you come up to bed?" Babs demanded. "I thought you'd gone out to look at the stars with Benny and Trux. But when they romped in, they had two other girls with them. Nick said he saw you running upstairs and sent me to find you." She sat down. "What on earth made you go to bed?"

Patricia, with her red hair in a sunrise effect about her face said, "I was sleepy."

"Weren't you having a good time?"

"Too swift for me, dearest. I haven't traveled as fast as you in the years since we saw each other."

Babs had a quick little sigh for that, then said, "But you ought to come down. We are having breakfast."

"Breakfast? What time is it?"

"Almost five."

"A.M.?"

"Yes."

"What time do you expect to get up tomorrow—or is it today?"

"In the afternoon. Trux and Benny are coming then to take us to a tea dance. They want you to go."

"But what about Toodles?"

"Toodles?"

"Yes. Won't he have any Christmas Day with you? Or Christmas dinner?"

"He will show me his stocking, and spend the day with Nonny. He'll be perfectly happy."

"Babs, don't you ever think how we loved Christmas morning, and our fathers and mothers being with us, and going to church, and all the children at dinner?"

"Nick says family gatherings are bromidic. He doesn't believe in such things."

"Don't you?"

"I'm not sure. And it's frightfully old-fashioned." Her voice took on a hard edge. "I'm not going to worry myself about it. I adore Nick." Trouble ahead for Babs! Patricia could hear Nick's voice saying, "If we love each other enough we'll stick it." If he did not love Babs enough, would he break her heart?

She reached out and caught Babs's hand in hers, "My dear, my dear," she said, "it isn't old-fashioned to have—faith!"

A voice in the hall. Nick's. "Babs, where are you?" Babs stood up. "Be a good sport, Patsy. You never used to be—stuffy. Come on down and be one of us."

The redheaded nurse, getting into her clothes, asked herself if being stuffy meant to want the best for Babs and her baby? Wishing happiness for them? Content?

She did not put on her party gown. She put on the dress she had worn when she came from the hospital. She looked up Nonny, and left a note with her. The note said, *"Babs, darling, I've got to go back. There's a blind boy at the hospital, and one who can't get well. And I think I ought to look after them. And you mustn't think I am stuffy, dearest. I am just the same Patsy who shared your room with you. And darling, if you ever need me, I'll come to the end of the earth."*

* * * * *

Doctor Jimmie Grant simply could not believe it. To have her in his arms. To hear her saying, "It was like waddling around with a lot of geese, after having flown with an eagle."

"Didn't you like it?"

"Like it? I *loathed* it. And I felt that I couldn't stay another minute. I went out to the garage and found a chauffeur who was glad enough to drive me over. And I couldn't get here quick enough. I kept thinking of what I wanted to tell you. I thought I might have to save it until later in the day—so we could be alone. And then the luck of it . . . to find you up and here."

"Here" was on the way to the hospital from the nurses' quarters. Patricia had gotten into white linen gown and cap and blue cape, and had started across the snowy way, and suddenly, there he was coming towards her, his head down and not seeing her! And she had come up to him in the Christmas dawn, and had clutched at his coat, and had said, continuing the conversation where it had ended the night before, "Jimmie, I don't want a rich husband. I want you."

He hadn't asked any questions, he had simply lifted her in his arms and said, "Thank God!" Time enough for questions when this supreme moment had passed. Time enough for everything . . . she was his forever.

It was bitterly cold, but they did not know it. Yet when they came into the hospital, he made her sit in his office, while she thawed out and he gave her an account of things that had happened.

"There's Pinkney's eyes," he said at last, "I saved that for you to tell him."

"He's going to get better?" But she knew from his voice.

"He's going to see."

She had risen in her chair and was looking at him, wide-eyed, vivid, wonderful, "Oh, Jimmie, Jimmie," she said, "to think that I thought I'd be happier eating scrambled eggs with all those idiots, than to be telling Pinkney . . ." Her voice failed her. "I'm going to cry," she said, "do you think it would be against discipline, if you would shut the door, and let me do it on your shoulder?"

The men in the ward felt there wasn't much to wake up for. Bruelle, restless with pain, had seen an hour ago the bright lights of a motorcar. He spoke now in a hushed voice to Pinkney. "Someone came in early."

"How do you know?"

"A car passed. A big one."

"What time is it?"

"Seven."

The night was over. But to Pinkney it would always be night. He sighed and covered up his head. Christmas morning? What did he care for Christmas!

Then suddenly there came to his ears a gay little tune! The tinkling from *The Magic Flute*! A music box!

He sat up, his ears strained to listen.

A murmur ran around the room, growing louder: "It's Miss Pat. She's back."

Pinkney simply couldn't believe it. Not even when she called out, "A merry Christmas, everybody," and shook hands all around, holding Pinkney's a little longer while she said, "I've got a present for you. Can you find your way to the sunroom in fifteen minutes?"

It was easy enough to find his way, and at this time, the room would be empty. He wondered what Miss Pat would give him for a present.

There was no sun at this hour, but he found the room warm. He sat in the big chair, listening for her step.

Patricia, coming in, said with seeming tactlessness: "Pinkney, I wish you could see the lovely sky."

His tone was dull. "I shall never see it."

"Pinkney, let me tell you about it." He knew from her voice that she was standing now by the wide window which faced the east, "Around the horizon is a strip of silver, and above that a strip of rose, and above that . . . above that . . . deep purple, with a star! . . . Pinkney, it's Christmas morning!"

Something moving now in her voice, something breathless, *"Pinkney . . ."*

She couldn't go on, and suddenly she began to sob. "Pinkney, you're going to *see*. The doctor says so. Next Christmas you are going to see the morning sky!"

His hand groped for her shoulder. Gripped it. He did not speak, but it was worth everything to catch his radiant, lifted look; worth all the glitter and gleam of golden oranges and bows and arrows, and green gowns and silver slippers. It was worth all the hard work she had ever done, and all the hard work that was yet to come—to see the radiance of his countenance as he turned his eyes up towards the coming light.

———————————

Temple Bailey was born in Petersburg, Virginia, and became one of the most popular—and highest paid—authors in the world during the first half of the twentieth century. Besides writing hundreds of stories that were published by the leading family magazines of her day, she also wrote books, such as *The Trumpeter Swan*, *The Holly Hedge*, and *The Wild Wind*.

The Missionary Barrel

Carolyn Abbot Stanley

The missionary barrel arrived in time for Christmas, but when they opened it, they wished they hadn't.
So what should they do with it?

* * * * *

John, have you gone to peddling—what's in your barrel?" John Haloran's wife threw open the door and called out into the wintry gale, as the frontier missionary drove up with a large barrel in the back of the wagon. He was numb with cold and fatigue, and answered absently, "Oh, I don't know, Mary."

"Well, I never saw one before, but my prophetic soul tells me this is a missionary barrel—and two days before Christmas. Hurray!"

She tried to be cheerful as she set the steaming supper before the weary man, but she knew without asking that the long overdue bank draft had not come. She kept the children busy in the kitchen playing menagerie while her husband ate in silence, but after a time he spoke.

"Mary, you've been doing the work of three women, the supplies are ever so low, it's Christmas, and the bank draft didn't come!"

"Never mind, this can't last forever. Maybe the draft will come next week. Those boys do eat so, but we have lots of potatoes left."

"It isn't just the money, it's the feeling of aloneness. Oh, if I could just feel that the church back there were doing all they could—were thinking of us. Sometimes I think they don't care!"

"Don't allow yourself to think that. Just look at this barrel. Would any church do this for us unless they know our work, and were trying to make it easier?"

After the children had been put to bed, Mrs. Haloran exclaimed, "Now, let's open the barrel."

"Our charity box," the minister called it bitterly.

"I can't help it, John, when I think of all the things these children need, I'm glad for the box."

The first thing to come out was a woman's hat box. For years Mary had worn a brown felt hat, trimmed with a knot of velvet. It was an annual process: this steaming the velvet and turning to a different angle; and now a vision of a black velvet hat floated through her mind. Her fingers trembled as she untied it.

"I'm glad the first thing is for you, Mary."

It was open at last, and she held it up to view an old leghorn hat, trimmed with faded, mashed flowers. Neither spoke for a minute, and then her sense of humor came to the rescue, and she put it on her head, saying, "We'll find something to go with it."

She found it, for next she produced an opera cloak of faded pink cloth, trimmed with moth-eaten swansdown.

"It's an outrage."

"Yes, it *is* an outrage, John, but it's funny."

39

Other garments about as useful were brought out until the barrel was empty.

"This is all—except this dear little suit, just right for Davie. And here is some writing. 'It was my little boy's that is gone.' Oh, John, we have Davie anyway, even if we haven't proper clothes for him. Poor, poor mother!"

A moment later, she was putting the garments back.

"It is a disappointment, but we certainly won't let it spoil our Christmas. I've made Paul an overcoat out of that old one of yours, and that gives each younger one a new coat, so everybody has a change. And out of the pieces that were left I made three mufflers to tie over their little heads as they scud across the prairies. And here are three pairs of mittens. I'm so proud of these mittens. And then the candy that you bought. Do you know, I've cut the family short on a pound of butter in order to have the candy; poor little dears, they are just starved for candy, but they shall have that, and it will ensure the children's good time. I'm going to fill the bags now—red tarleton from a peach basket. John, get the candy."

The moment which John Haloran had been dreading had come.

"Mary, I didn't get the candy."

"You didn't get it?"

"No, I used the money to finish paying the freight on the barrel."

40

"John Haloran, you didn't! The children's candy money that I've been hoarding up for months. Why, John, Davie has been praying for that candy."

"What could I do, Mary? They wouldn't let me have the box without it, and I supposed there would be presents for the children!"

"For one dollar we could have given them a Christmas they never would have forgotten. It would have bought them a book and toy apiece, and two pounds of ten cent candy— and our children would have thought that was glorious. Poor little dears."

She had been speaking in a low voice, then she suddenly said, "There's nothing right or fair about it. I'll tell you the kind of women they are. They go up and down the streets saying to every acquaintance they meet, 'Do tell me what to get for my boy.' He has everything in the world! And just think! I'd be satisfied with a dollar for my four!"

The missionary was speechless before her wrath.

"This barrel is going back tomorrow. I'm going to give those people a lesson they won't forget."

* * * * *

It was about two weeks after this that the pastor of the First Church announced that a full attendance was desired at the missionary meeting to take action about a barrel that had been returned—not only returned, but refused. The president of the society hoped for a large attendance—and she got it. Never had there been such a meeting. She stood, cleared her throat, and looked out at the full church.

"Ladies, I feel called upon to explain. At our October meeting, it was decided to send a box to our missionary in the west. I was called out of town, but I left a list of the needs and the address with another. You will remember that the barrel was sent out as an offering—a Christmas offering from the First Church, not the missionary society alone, but our wealthy First Church. It was returned immediately, and with it came this letter which I shall read. This is from Mrs. John Haloran, the missionary's wife, and I am told by a friend of hers in our church that she is a cultured and refined woman. I found out before leaving that they had four boys ranging in ages from five to eleven—so there would be no haphazard, misfit giving. I left the directions with one of the members."

"Madam President, I had the papers; I simply forgot to send them to the society," volunteered an embarrassed woman.

"It has placed us in a mortifying position. It exemplifies the old saying:

'Evil is wrought by want of thought
As well as want of heart.'

"The letter reads as follows:

"My Dear Madam: The barrel so generously sent by the First Church is received, and contents carefully noted. After prayerful consideration of our wardrobe, I find we are not in need of the articles contained in it, so am returning it this early so that it may be used in discharging the obligations of the First Church to some of its other missionaries. If sent to the right party—say a missionary's wife whose spirit has not already been crushed by the burdens of frontier life, I should say that it might be used several times for this purpose.

"I add a little contribution in the way of scripture texts, which will enhance the value of your gifts. The home missionary is so used to subsisting on the Word of God that he may feed on these and be filled. Likewise, it may also clothe him with the garment of praise. And is it too much to hope that they may do good in the household of faith to them that are in the First Church?

Very sincerely yours,
Mary C. Haloran"

"Well, I don't see as it tells us why it was returned," said an obtuse member.

"The barrel will explain itself," added the president. "We will take an inventory and listen to the scripture messages. The secretary will please read."

She drew from the barrel the same promising box that we saw before, handed the slip to Mrs. Willman as she held up the leghorn hat.

"God loveth a cheerful giver." There was a burst of laughter in which the donor joined.

Next came a child's hat, trimmed with old forget-me-nots.

"He that hath pity upon the poor lendeth unto the LORD." And the president added, "Just how many loans of this kind He needs I'm not sure. Not many, I should hope."

Then she held up a man's dust-grimed straw hat, and the secretary read, "And the Levite that is within thy gates, thou shalt not forsake him."

They were not smiling now, and whispers of, "Who on earth sent those things?" were heard all around.

"Shh—look at that, will you?" and the president was holding up to view the pink cloth opera cloak, and there floated out over the audience a cloud of swansdown that set them all coughing as the secretary read, "Lay up for yourselves treasures in heaven, where neither moth nor rust doth consume, and where thieves do not break through nor steal." It was not in human nature not to laugh at that, but a woman with a sealskin coat stared straight ahead of her.

"Madam President, is there nothing fit to wear in that barrel?"

"Yes, there are those two beautiful winter dresses and some baby clothes for the Haloran boys. The next is a contribution to the minister himself." And the secretary read,

"If there be with thee a poor man, one of thy brethren, . . . thou . . . shalt surely lend him sufficient for his need." And the president held up to view two old vests.

The First Church was beginning to see what a gratuitous insult it had offered, for the First Church was well-bred. The packing had been done at a time when closets were being cleared for the winter and the bundles and packages were dumped into the missionary barrel, but the scripture texts elucidated the law of sacrifice with startling clearness.

"Ladies, I'm glad to say that this text is the last, and I beg that the First Church will take it as a message from Him whom we serve: 'Thou shalt not oppress an hired servant that is poor and needy, . . . in his day thou shalt give him his hire, neither shall the sun go down upon it.' Deuteronomy twenty-four verses fourteen and fifteen."

Before Mrs. McArthur had finished, the treasurer was on her feet.

"At last we're at the root of the matter. No, mark my words, the man's salary has not been paid, and his wife is smarting under the injustice that we should try to supply that deficiency with a barrel of rags."

"Well, I should like to know what we have a board for if it isn't to attend to these affairs," said a well-groomed woman.

"Well, the board cannot honestly pay out what we have not paid in."

The president rapped for order. "I have not finished this letter. Mrs. Haloran says, 'I return the barrel with one exception, the little suit with these words: "It was my little boy's that is gone,"—and I cried over that little suit, and I accept it as from a sister, and may the Lord comfort that dear sad heart.' "

The mother in black covered her face with her hands, and a hush fell on the whole company. Slowly the president added, "Ladies, I also have a letter written by Mrs. Haloran the following day. She says,

"My Dear Madam: After a night of self-abasement, I write to tell you how deeply I regret my action of yesterday, and how gladly I would recall it if I could. I could not have kept the things, but it was an ignoble use to make of the blessed Word of God. I will only say in excuse that we needed warm clothing, but my husband's salary was so long overdue, and we just could not bring ourselves to go into debt."

"That's just what I thought!" exclaimed the treasurer.

"So you can imagine how like mockery this barrel seemed to me when we even had to use the children's candy money to finish paying the freight on the barrel."

"Oh! Oh! For shame!" came from all over the house.

"What I did was against my husband's earnest entreaties. I know now that he was right, but, oh! if the church at home could only be brought to see that what we need is not charity but honest pay.

Yours,
Mary C. Haloran"

"I have never been so humiliated in my life," said the president. "The thing I most deeply deplore and cannot understand is why that barrel should have been sent without paying the freight. I left my personal check as a contribution for that very purpose.

"And I have just returned it to you. I forgot it until today, and anyway, I thought they ought to be glad to pay the freight on a valuable box," volunteered one tight-lipped woman.

"Do *you* send Christmas gifts in that way?" There was no answer.

"Well, ladies, what shall we do with this barrel?"

"Madam President, out of the mouth of this barrel we stand convicted of selfish indifference toward those we have promised to stand by. I move that we send this family a box that shall be worthy of this church, and commensurate with their needs."

There were a dozen seconds, but the president doubted if it would be accepted or not.

"Well, I've learned a lesson that will last me all the rest of my life," said the lady who had sent the opera cloak. "I would like to say as much in a note tucked into the pocket of a warm, new cloak for the minister."

The building was lively now, and even the treasurer said, "You all know that I am not in favor of missionary barrels. They are too often a substitute for the salary we haven't paid. But I've got to put in five pounds of candy, if all my principles go to smash."

"And I would like to say that I will pack that box," said the lady who had sent the former one, "and pay the freight as a trespass offering."

Then the plainspoken treasurer took the floor. "Madam President, I want to say that as we leave here we will feel very self-righteous. This box is sent in a spasm of generosity, as the other was sent in a spasm of indifference, but let me tell you that nothing worth while is supported by spasms. If any of you see that the time has come to pay dollars instead of duds, hold up your pocketbooks." From all over the house went up bags of silver, leather, and filigree.

"Thank the Lord! Your conversion is genuine, but give me your checks before you go."

The beaming president arose. "You have disposed of the situation beautifully, ladies, but the barrel remains. What shall we do with the barrel?"

"Madam President, we have had our thank offerings, our trespass offerings, and any number of freewill offerings; I move that we make this barrel a burnt offering!"

And so they did.

Carolyn Abbot Stanley wrote for magazines during the early part of the twentieth century.

The Christmas Rose

Marlene J. Chase

Life . . . love . . . even marriage seemed to have lost its savor—even its meaning. In fact, she even dreaded Christmas itself.

Then—"Excuse me, Miss."

* * * * *

A light snow was falling as she turned the key to open Rose's Flower Shop. The name didn't take much imagination, but then it was better than "Rosie's Posies" as Clint had suggested when she had first begun the business.

"Going to the Towers again this year?" asked Cass Gunther, who was opening up the European deli next door.

Rose nodded. It was what they did every year. Supper and drinks at the club and Christmas Eve at Huntingdon's posh Park Towers. They'd swim, relax in the hot tub—maybe take in a show. It was a tradition, but one she had to admit had lost its luster somehow.

She turned on the lights, feeling bone tired. People would wait until the last minute to place their Christmas orders, she supposed, and she'd have to scramble to fill them. Why did she do it every year? It wasn't that she needed the money, but it filled her days and the business had gone well. Then, too, there was something soothing about working with flowers.

"I'll be home for Christmas . . ." the sentimental lyric rose from the radio under the counter. A wave of sadness or homesickness swept over her. Home was four extravagantly decorated walls, which she welcomed at the end of the day, but when it came down to it, what was there for her really? Perhaps if they'd been able to have children . . .

They'd had a reasonably good marriage, the best house on Carriage Drive, money in the bank, and enough friends to keep them from feeling lonely. And goodness knows they were too busy to think about whether or not they were happy. The bills for the mortgage, the car and boat, and a half dozen credit cards never stopped.

Rose sighed, aware of a hollow place inside her. She supposed she wasn't the only one who experienced melancholy at Christmas. What should be a celebration had become drudgery, a pause in the year's calendar that interrupted schedules and left one vaguely aware that something was missing in their tedious lives. Even anticipating Clint's surprise when he unwrapped the Pendleton sport coat she'd bought held little joy. His gift to her would be something beautiful, expensive, she supposed, but she couldn't remember last year's gift or when they had taken time to really talk to each other. She felt suddenly at odds with the whole world, cross.

Perhaps if they'd kept up with the family. But family meant Clint's two aunts in Virginia and her stepfather in Wyoming, none of who seemed famished for their company. Hungry, that was it. In the rush to get to the shop, she'd forgotten to eat breakfast. The deli was right next door, but even the smell of freshly roasted coffee and bagels held little enticement.

The bell over the door announced a customer, but she kept her back to the counter and consulted the order book. She wasn't ready for the world of people yet.

"Excuse me, Miss," an elderly voice called from behind her.

I haven't been a Miss for fourteen years, thank you. She swallowed the caustic retort and turned slowly to find an old man smiling at her.

He had all his teeth, a full head of wavy white hair and a look of kind apology. Across his chest, he held a plaid cap, and he gave her a quaint little bow like an aging Sir Galahad. "I'm looking for some flowers—for my wife."

At those words, something luminous lit him from within. He was like a little boy buying a cherished gift for his mother, or like a young suitor eager to please a beautiful maiden. She wondered if Clint ever looked that way when he spoke about her. "I see," she said slowly, waiting.

The man tapped gnarled fingers over his cap in meditation and, with warm authority in his raspy voice, said, "Not just any flowers. They must be Christmas roses."

"Well, we have roses. We have 'American Beauty' reds, pink, tea, and yellow—"

"Oh, no," he said, shifting his negligible weight from one foot to the other in a kind of anticipatory dance. "Christmas roses—white as snow—with some of the feathery ferns tucked in. And I'd like a big red bow too."

"It's Christmas Eve, sir, and I'm afraid we're fresh out—"

"My wife loves white roses," he continued, looking at something she couldn't see. "They remind her of the Babe of Christmas and the purity of His heart. She hasn't seen any roses for such a long time. And now that she . . ."

The old man's shoulders drooped ever so slightly, and then straightened again. Rose heard the faint tremor and was touched by something beautiful in the old face that made her think of alabaster. No, alabaster was too cold.

"She's ill now . . ." He paused and tucked his cap under his arm. "We served at a medical clinic in West Africa for more than thirty years. But we've had to return home. Nell has Alzheimer's. We've living at Country Gardens."

"Oh, I'm sorry," Rose breathed.

The man rushed on without a trace of bitterness. "I have a little room on the floor just below the nursing wing where Nell is. We share meals together—and we have our memories. God has been good to us."

Rose returned his smile, uncomprehending, but unable to deny the man's sincerity. White roses on Christmas Eve? She might be able to get them from Warrensville, but it would be a stretch.

"We'll be spending Christmas Eve in my room—just the two of us. A celebration," he was saying. "Christmas roses for Nell would make it perfect." He stood, cap in hand, brows lifted, his feet still doing their almost imperceptible little dance.

"I may be able to get them sent over from Warrensville." Rose bit her lip. Was she crazy? It would take a miracle. Then there was the price. It would cost a fortune, and this man looked like he didn't have two nickels to rub together. "How much do you want to spend?"

The man set his cap on the counter and dug out a faded wallet from trousers that had seen several winters. He pushed four five dollar bills toward her with childlike eagerness, then seeing her dismay, hesitated. "I hope it's enough."

"I could give you a nice spray of red roses in a bud vase," Rose began. White rose centerpieces started at thirty-five dollars. Then the delivery charge would run another twenty, especially on Christmas Eve. If she could even get them!

"I had hoped for a real special bouquet . . ." He broke off, and she read his profound disappointment.

"Leave it to me. I'll do my best to get you something nice," she began, astounded by her own words. She'd made a hasty promise to an old missionary she didn't even know. This was not the Rose McThadden she knew!

"Bless you!" the old man said, reaching across the counter and grasping her hands. "Can they be delivered around four or five o'clock? That's when we're having our Christmas together—Nell and I. It will be such a surprise! Oh, I can't thank you enough." Nearly dancing, he replaced his cap and began backing toward the door. "Arnold Herriman—room seven! Merry Christmas! God bless you! God bless you!"

What had a tired old man with a sick wife to be so happy about? She puzzled over that through a hasty breakfast and the next several orders. Then placed a call to a supplier in Warrensville. They could get her a dozen white roses at forty-two dollars and fifty cents, but it would be four o'clock before they could be relayed to her shop. Then there was the matter of the "feathery ferns and the big red bow," and time for her to put it all together in some semblance of a bouquet.

"OK," she said wearily, realizing that she herself would have to deliver the Christmas roses to Mr. Herriman. No matter. Clint would likely be delayed by a promising client.

The flowers arrived at ten minutes to four and Rose quickly arranged them in a silver bowl, tucking in the feathery greens and sprigs of baby's breath and holly. She secured a lacy red bow around the base and balanced it in one hand while locking the door with the other.

Country Gardens hardly resembled its name. Surely a couple who'd spent a lifetime healing the sick in an obscure village deserved better in the sunset of their years.

She found the residential wing and tentatively approached #7. Arnold Herriman in the same old trousers and shirt with a crimson tie, beamed at her. She entered a room with a few pieces of old furniture and walls bursting with pictures and certificates. There were beaming faces of African children, carved elephants, tigers, and a beaded banner. On the hall table against a brilliantly painted fabric was a crèche. *The Babe of Christmas and the purity of His heart,* Herriman had said. Rose tore her eyes away and followed Arnold Herriman into the living room.

A diminutive woman sat on the sofa with hands folded over a patchwork quilt on her lap. She had a translucent complexion and vacant blue eyes above two brightly rouged cheeks. A bit of red ribbon had been tucked into her white hair. When she saw the flowers, her eyes widened and quickly spilled over with tears.

"Nell, darling. It's your surprise—Christmas roses," Arnold said, placing an arm around the woman's fragile shoulders.

"Oh, how lovely!" Nell stretched out her arms to the bouquet, her face transformed in radiance. She rubbed one wrinkled cheek against the delicate petals and turned a watery gaze on Rose. "Do I know you, dear?"

"This is the nice lady from the flower shop who made your bouquet," Arnold said.

"Can you stay a while, dear?" she asked. "We'll be finished with our patients soon and we'll take you to our house for tea."

"Oh, no . . ." said Rose.

Arnold touched his wife's shoulder. "The patients are all gone, dear. We're home, and it's Christmas Eve."

Rose's throat ached with unshed tears and the sense that something beautiful lived here from which she was excluded. Could it be that in living their lives for others these two old people who had nothing but each other and a bouquet of white roses had everything that was important?

Suddenly, Nell plucked one of the long-stemmed white roses from the elegant bouquet and held it out to Rose. "Please, I have so many. You must take one for yourself!"

"Yes," Arnold said, taking the stem from his wife and pressing it toward her. "Thank you for all your trouble. God bless you."

She wanted to say that He already had blessed her beyond understanding, that bringing them the Christmas roses had made her happier than she could remember in a long time, that on this Christmas Eve she had learned something of the meaning of the holiday she had missed until now.

Lt. Col. Marlene J. Chase retired in 2006 from her appointment as editor in chief and literary secretary for the Salvation Army Publications in the United States. Besides having served as an ordained minister for forty-three years, she is a prolific writer. Her writings have been published in magazines and short story collections around the world, and she has authored seven books. Today, she lives and writes from Rockford, Illinois.

Through the Mike

Ruth Herrick Myers

Camilla ought to be happy, had she not written the already acclaimed script for the Christmas play? Instead, she was miserable—deadly jealous of her more popular sister, Rosie. She just didn't see how she could take it anymore.
Then came the dead microphone.

* * * * *

Camilla fixed her attention upon the Christmas wreath in the dean's window and tried to keep her mind upon what the dean was saying.

"You don't seem as enthusiastic as I imagined you would be, Camilla."

"Oh, yes," insisted Camilla. *Sparkle up,* she told herself. *Can't you even show a polite interest in the idea?* "Rosie and I have been planning on the trip for a long time, partly because Hazleton was Mother's alma mater, and partly because it really is the college we both like best."

Dean Wilde looked at Camilla keenly. "Well, that's splendid. I'll put you both down tentatively then for the weekend at Hazleton between semesters. Twins ought to create quite a commotion in the freshman class. I remember there were twins who were sophomores when I was a college freshman."

Camilla heard herself ask, "Did they stay together all through college?"

Again that questioning look in Miss Wilde's eyes. "No, they separated at the end of two years and finished in different universities."

Well, she certainly couldn't blame them for that, Camilla was thinking unhappily. She realized that her business with the dean was over. Rising, she said, "Thank you very much for taking care of it for us, Miss Wilde, and Merry Christmas, if I don't see you again."

"Merry Christmas, Camilla. I hear the continuity you wrote for the pageant tomorrow is very delightful."

"I loved writing it," said Camilla, touched. At least it was consoling to have somebody remember her part in it. Especially since Rosie seemed to be stealing the show completely at the moment.

It was too bad to feel so unmerry right at Christmastime, but that was exactly the state of Camilla Alden's mind as she left the dean's office and headed for the assembly hall. Rosie would be there managing things as chairman of the production committee. No wonder the girls were crazy about her, Camilla reflected. Rosie was so capable, such a keen executive. Look what clever ideas she had had about all the costumes. The shepherds in their soft blue and dusty rose robes were perfect. The turbans of the wise men were an achievement. And all at practically no cost to the Girls' Club, which was putting on the pageant for the benefit of their little guests, the Seabury Settlement children. Rosie had just utilized people's bathrobes and scarfs and dirndls and made something out of practically nothing.

Camilla opened the assembly room door. No one would pay any attention to her, though, if she did go in, she thought miserably. And hated herself for such a hideous attitude. Why

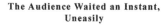

couldn't she be broad-minded about it? People just naturally liked Rosie better, and that was all there was to it. The reason it was so noticeable was that they were twins—not identical twins to be sure, but twins, for all that, and therefore always being compared one with the other.

But Camilla saw as soon as she entered the hall that there was something wrong. Everybody looked glum and worried. Up on the platform was Rosie—stumped, for once.

"It won't do," Camilla heard Rosie say. "There'll be a lot of noise in the audience anyhow, with all the kids shuffling their feet and wiggling around. We just have to have people hear you, Loree, or the whole thing will fall flat."

"If someone else's voice is better than mine, go ahead and have her do it," offered Loree. "I won't mind a bit, really."

"It's not your voice," Rosie said dubiously. "It's just the wretched acoustics in this hall. Oh, dear, why can't we have a new high school, I wonder."

"For this pageant at least," Loree laughed. "Dot, you try and see if your voice carries better. Someone ought to go back— Oh, there's Camilla. Listen, Camilla, see if you can hear Dot, will you?"

"Shoot!" Camilla called back.

The shepherds settled themselves again in their places. Dot took the paper and read from Camilla's continuity, "And there were shepherds abiding in the field . . ."

Camilla stood listening at the back of the room. Rosie stood listening over by the windows.

**The Audience Waited an Instant,
Uneasily**

50

No one would have known they were twins. Camilla Alden was tall like Aunt Bertie, a New England aunt, and as reserved and bottled up as Aunt Bertie too. She was an appreciative and habitual reader: books were her life. People just naturally accepted the fact that Camilla could do the best continuity, the best themes in English class, or the best bit of incidental poetry.

Rosie, on the other hand, was a blue-eyed blonde, "a bit on the chubby side," as Camilla put it affectionately. If Rosie was impetuous, she was also courageous and original. If she was quick-tempered, she was also as instantly penitent. And when it came to working with her hands, there was just nothing Rosie couldn't do—and do better than anyone else.

No, she just couldn't take it all through college too, Camilla was thinking as she stood watching Rosie. Four years of college, as there had been four years of high school. Four more years of watching Rosie and admiring her and knowing that people were thinking, *How much more clever Rosie is than Camilla!* Four more years of wondering why people always liked Rosie best and what she could do about it.

Rosie called out suddenly, "You're not a bit better, Dot. Listen! I've got a simply swell idea. I'm going over to Dr. Poole's study and see if he'll let us borrow the church amplifiers for tomorrow."

Camilla gasped. "Rosie! You wouldn't!"

"Why not?"

"Why, those amplifiers are just his angel children!"

"Better yet. They ought to work just as well here as in the church. He can't do less than turn us down. I'm going right over. Wait for me, kids."

No one but Rosie would have thought of such a thing. But she'd probably come back with Dr. Poole's amplifiers and his blessing, to boot, mused Camilla.

She did. More than that, Dr. Poole had packed up the amplifiers for Rosie and brought them over to the high school for her in his own car. He was tremendously popular with the young people of his church and Rosie was proud to introduce him to all the girls as her minister. Dr. Poole was making a definite hit, Camilla observed.

"It's certainly lovely of you to let us take them," Camilla told him warmly. "I do hope nothing happens to them."

"If anything does, Rosie can fix it, I have no doubt," Dr. Poole laughed. He was still young enough himself to be enthusiastic about things, and the Alden twins were rather pets of his—especially Rosie, Camilla knew. Or thought she knew. Once Dr. Poole had surprised her as she was watching Rosie, with the remark, "Comparisons are odious, aren't they, Camilla?" And had looked at her with the same quizzical gaze as the dean's this afternoon.

Goodness! thought Camilla, now uneasy. *When I look at Rosie do I look jealous, or what?*

Dr. Poole helped the girls assemble the amplifier and set it up.

"I like the microphone to this set," said Rosie. "It's so inconspicuous." It did stand up, two little posts, one at each side of the speaker's stand, in a harmless sort of way that certainly should give no speaker stage fright. "Usually," said Rosie, "the mike is a round sort of thing. This is much nicer," she said with satisfaction. "Wasn't it grand of Dr. Poole to let us take it?"

"You're sure you know how it works?" queried Camilla, still worried. "So that if anything goes wrong—"

"Leave it to me," said Rosie. "There is a bad spot in that

one length of wire. But Dr. Poole and I decided it wouldn't break yet."

"What would happen if it did break?"

Rosie laughed. "It just wouldn't loud-speak any more, darling," she said in amusement. "Someday you'll learn, Camilla."

The girls standing around all laughed, and Camilla felt her cheeks grow red.

* * * * *

A more Christmasy afternoon could not have been ordered than the afternoon of the Girls' Club Christmas pageant and party for the Seabury Settlement children. At noon it had started to snow, and now at half past two, it was coming down in great big feathery flakes, to the intense joy of the boys and girls.

The assembly hall looked lovely. Colored panels at the back of the platform gave the impression of stained glass windows in a cathedral. At each side in front, partially concealing the amplifiers, stood a lighted Christmas tree. Presently the red velvet curtains would be lowered to allow the first tableau to take its place, but Camilla had decided that the first impression should be that of the Christmas cathedral. And the children's upturned, expectant faces proved to her that her choice had been a wise one.

Camilla sat back in the audience to listen with the rest. Her work was over. There were numerous scenes, all portraying the Christmas story—the coming of the wise men, the appearance of the angels to the shepherds abiding in the field, the lovely scene in the stable of the inn with Mary bending low over the manger where a faint light glowed.

The programs merely announced that the continuity was written by Camilla Alden. *That was all there was to show for her hard work,* Camilla thought. And she wished again that she might have been more like Rosie: popular, cheerful, always in the midst of things, instead of being aloof, remote, one who always seemed to do her work alone.

She felt suddenly lonely, unmerry again. She had just about decided not to try to go through college with Rosie after all. Let Rosie go to Hazelton. Rosie was like Mother anyhow. She would be popular at Hazelton, Camilla knew. She'd be president of the freshman class or something like that the first thing. She couldn't miss.

As for herself, Camilla decided, she'd like to go anywhere where there wouldn't be always this dreadful comparison between the quiet twin and the lively twin, the pretty blond one and the dark serious one. *Is that what people said about them,* Camilla often wondered. *It was true,* Camilla told herself, facing the facts in all honesty.

The curtains were drawn now around the platform and the announcer's stand. The lights were dimmed. A hush fell over the audience. As the curtains parted again for the first tableau, even Camilla felt the thrill of a great achievement. The wise men were kneeling in the desert, gazing at the star. One spoke.

Loree's voice came sweetly and clearly through the amplifiers. The effect was perfect, the children still as mice. When the curtain fell at last there was only a great hush. No one clapped. Camilla was glad of that. It was exactly the effect she had hoped the tableau might produce.

One after another the scenes were run off. All was going beautifully, even better than Camilla had dreamed. And then, suddenly, just as the shepherds in the field should begin to hear the song of the angels—the amplifiers went dead!

It must be that wire, after all, thought Camilla. The audience waited an instant, uneasily. Then the curtains dropped and Loree pushed her way through them to speak to the audience.

"There's the slight matter of a broken wire," explained Loree. "If you will be patient just a minute, I'm sure we can have it fixed."

The audience waited. In about five minutes, the amplifiers started to speak again—but from a most different script!

"The Alden twins are swell, aren't they?" one girlish voice said.

"Aren't they!" said another voice. "I never thought I'd like to be twins; but if I could still be individuals as they are, I think it would be fun."

"I'll say," said still a third voice. "They aren't a bit alike, but who wants to be a rubber stamp of anybody's twin sister? I think Camilla's really going to be famous someday. Did you know that Miss Barlow read her continuity in English yesterday? All the teachers were talking about it."

"They're so loyal to each other," another girl said. "That's what I like about them. You'd think they'd be jealous of each other sometimes: they're both so good in their own lines; but one just seems to supplement the other. You can't imagine Rosie with Camilla or Camilla without—"

Then a horrified voice cried, "Girls—*hush*! Do you know that everything you're saying is being broadcast right out into the audience?" Rosie got the wire fixed and plugged the switch in again.

Then—dead silence!

The audience, for one hectic minute, rocked with laughter. Then the curtains parted upon the same shepherds in the field and the pageant went on, with Loree's voice reading the lines once more.

Camilla, leaning forward in her seat, felt a sudden weight—the weight of years—roll off. Was that what people *really* said about her and Rosie? Why, it must be! They really had said it. They really had said that everyone liked them *both*! That everyone thought they were *both* good! That, even though different, one seemed to supplement the other!

Why, that meant, then, that they could both go to Hazelton; that there was room for both of them in the various college activities; that she need never worry anymore about what people were saying.

A flood of joy poured into Camilla's heart. The shepherds were looking up into the Christmas sky. Somewhere the songs of the angels began to be heard. "It came upon a midnight clear, that glorious song of old . . ."

Camilla, sitting there alone in the dark with shining eyes, was singing with the angels.

Ruth Herrick Myers wrote for inspirational magazines during the first half of the twentieth century.

One Christmas Eve

Frank Bennett

Like most really good teachers, his students became part of his life, and he couldn't help taking their choices personally. Here was Ann, lovely and a little naive about the world, preparing to take a step that could destroy her future happiness.

What should he do?

* * * * *

No use denying it, the girl worried me. Choir rehearsal was over, and the others had gone, laughing and joking like college kids do the week before Christmas vacation.

But not Ann Stafford. Of course, she had to stay to pick up and sort out the music. She was my librarian: the job paid a little, and she needed money.

The late afternoon sun came through the high windows of the music hall, long strips of pale light that seemed to find all the hidden traces of copper in Ann's soft, light-brown hair.

She wasn't a very tall girl. Slender, with a nice figure and a lovely oval face that was meant to show off a certain kind of smile. The kind that begins as a twinkle in a girl's clear, honest eyes and works its way along her smooth cheeks to the corners of her mouth. But today, Ann wasn't smiling.

"One more rehearsal, the concert, and then vacation," I said cheerfully. "Going home, I suppose?"

"No." She dropped a bundle of music on the table. I picked up a piece of music and pretended to concentrate on it. But I was watching Ann. She belonged to the educational department—studying to be a teacher and sang in my choir just because she liked to sing—so she was really none of my affair. But I asked, "How come you're not going home?"

She shrugged. "Eddie's band has a few engagements during vacation, and it's a chance for me to earn some extra money."

Even though it wasn't any of my business, still I didn't like that. A nice girl like Ann Stafford singing with Eddie Fowler's Madcats. But Ann was twenty. She was old enough to know her way around.

As for Eddie—well, at the last faculty meeting, he'd been the subject of a long discussion. He was one of the few flunkers and troublemakers who wasn't coming back to Iowa State next semester.

Ann glanced up from the music, a small unhappy smile touching her lips. "I suppose I could go home for Christmas Day," she added. "But it seems a little foolish to spend so much on train fare for such a short visit."

* * * * *

Vaguely I knew how it was with Ann, the oldest of a large family, earning whatever she could to help pay her own way. I put the music down, and then said, "I'm driving to Council Bluffs the day before Christmas. Going to play the new organ at the St. James Church in a Christmas Eve dedication service. Don't you live near Fairdale, on the way to Council Bluffs?"

She nodded; and I went on casually, "Just the wife and I are going—there'll be plenty of room—and then you could ride back to Ames with us the day after Christmas."

Her smile was suddenly as warm as a summer day. "Oh, wonderful!" she said. "Thank you, Mr. Lewis. Thanks so much."

"We'll count on you," I said, pulled on my overcoat and stepped out into the corridor.

A tall, thin young man with slicked-down black hair ran into me.

"Sorry, Mr. Lewis," he said curtly.

"Hello, Eddie," I tried to speak pleasantly. "How are you?"

Eddie Fowler played a saxophone, not good, not bad, but he had a knack of faking that seemed to please the dancers. He gave me a sour glance. Two years ago, when he'd first come to Ames, he'd sung in my choir. But he'd never been dependable, so finally I'd had to check him out.

"Oh," he said, "I'm OK. Is Ann still here?"

"Sorting the music," I answered and went on outside.

* * * * *

I liked it less and less, Ann tying up with Eddie. Thinking about it, it seemed to me that there must be more to it than her singing with the band, for she wasn't the jazz-singer type. She had the kind of voice—clear, sweet, soft—that seems right for lullabies and hymns.

Arriving home, I said something to Kate about Ann's singing with the Madcats; and Kate shook her head.

"You never know what's going on, do you?" she said. "Eddie's been rushing Ann all winter. I've even heard they're practically engaged."

Just then, the phone rang. It was the dean asking Kate and me to chaperone a sorority dance. Of course, we were glad to. Besides, Eddie's Madcats played for this dance, and I wanted to get a better look at this whole situation.

Ann was up on the stage with the band, lovely to look at and smiling, but not quite sure of herself, somehow.

"Whatever became of that boy she used to date?" Kate whispered as we danced our way past the stage. "Stanley something-or-other, wasn't it?"

I'd forgotten about the boy, Stanley Arnold—he hadn't returned to college this year. I'd never known him very well, although he had a good tenor voice and had been in my choir.

Now, I recalled he had been taking courses in animal husbandry. A country boy, quiet, nice manners. He and Ann had known each other since high school and always seemed to have a lot of fun together.

"I'm going to ask Ann about him."

"You'd better keep your nose out of it," Kate advised. But she didn't really mean it.

After our last choir rehearsal, I played some Bach on the organ, while Ann was gathering up the music. In the mirror, I saw her stop her work occasionally to listen.

I stopped playing and said conversationally, "That's something I'm planning to play on the new organ in Council Bluffs."

"It's beautiful," she said softly. "Bach, isn't it?"

I nodded, and then said, "All set for the trip home?"

"Yes. I had a letter from Mother this morning. She and Joe and the kids are all happy about it."

"Joe?"

"Joe Miller, my stepfather. I've always called him Joe."

That seemed to break the ice, for after that it wasn't hard to get her to talk about her family. Her father had died when she was quite young, and when she was eight, her mother had married Joe Miller. Ann now had three half brothers and a half sister.

* * * * *

They're swell kids," she said, her eyes shining. "Jeanie's the baby—three last month. She's a little doll. Red curly hair and blue eyes and dimples. Max is the oldest. Eleven. Crazy about outdoor things."

It was easy to keep her talking now. About the bad luck, the hospital bills that had kept the Millers down.

"Mother and Joe have already done so much for me," she said. "That's why I'm trying to make my own way in college—Mr. Lewis." She lifted her slim shoulders, "I should tell you now so you can find someone to take my place next semester. I'm going to quit school. Eddie's quitting too. He's going to reorganize his band and go on the road. He's asking me to go along. To sing—"

I could have told her that he was quitting school only because he was about to get kicked out. But I didn't.

"It's my big chance to do something with my voice," she said. "Eddie says that after a year or so on the road, we'll be ready for radio, television, recordings—then I can repay Joe and help the kids go to college and—"

* * * * *

Well, I'm not so sure about—" I saw her begin to freeze up, and let it go at that.

"Say," I said as if I'd just thought of it, "I've been going to ask you—whatever became of Stanley Arnold? I miss him in the choir this year. Tenors are hard to find."

"Oh, Stan," she said his name too casually. "He couldn't come this year. His dad hurt his back pretty badly, and Stan had to stay home to look after the farm. Sometimes I think he likes that better, anyway. I guess the only reason he came was because his folks wanted him to."

Or because you came, I thought. Aloud, I said, "Seemed like a nice boy."

She didn't add anything to that, but began to sort the music.

"You and Stanley have trouble?" I asked.

She smiled. It wasn't a very big smile. "Oh, no. It's just that—well, he's back home, and I'm here. You know how it is—well, he's pretty busy, and I worked in Council Bluffs last summer, and now this winter—"

* * * * *

At that moment, Eddie Fowler came into the room. "Hurry it up, Ann," he said irritably. "We're waiting for you to try those new numbers."

"All right, Eddie," she said; and I went stamping out into the snow.

I was furious with them both. Eddie wasn't going any place except down.

But how could I make her understand this. If I told her in so many words I'd probably lose every bit of confidence and trust she had in me. I decided to keep still. For a while, at least.

In spite of the snowstorm that evening, a lot of kids came out for our annual Christmas concert. They sang great, and I was proud of them.

The next morning, it was still snowing when we picked up Ann at her rooming house, but the roads were not bad.

At noon, we stopped at a small town to eat. I tried to pay for Ann's lunch, but she wouldn't have it. Instead, she insisted on paying the whole check. "Please, Mr. Lewis," she said. "It's such a small thing for letting me ride home with you."

I got out of that one by telling her that the college always paid my expenses when I went out of town to play.

* * * * *

We hadn't gone another mile before the wind shifted and the storm really let loose. Soon the big flakes were jamming the windshield wipers. The highway became slick in spots and drifted with snow in other places. I glanced at Kate. She looked worried.

"Let's hear what the radio says," she said finally.

I switched it on. A moment later, the announcer broke into the program with storm warnings. Dangerous driving. Stay off the highways. Blizzard moving in. And so on.

We came to a car that had skidded into a ditch, with the man, his wife, and two kids in it. We helped them get on their way again, and we both eased along at a snail's pace. If there were any houses along that stretch of road, you couldn't see them for the blinding snow.

Plowing through the drifts was draining the gas tank at an alarming rate, but we were lucky. We managed to keep going until we reached Fairdale.

I pulled up in the protection of a building and stopped. "This is as far as we're going," I said.

"There's no hotel here," Ann said. "But my home's not much further on. Mother and Joe would be glad to put you up until the roads are cleared, I know."

I glanced at Kate. She looked tired, and I was ready to call it a day myself. "Thanks, Ann," I said. "Looks like you're stuck with us for the night."

* * * * *

It was only a quarter of a mile on to the Miller farm, and I don't think I'll ever forget how wonderful it was to see that big old square house. And the Millers themselves.

Ann's mother came to the door—a small, plump woman with a quiet, contented expression in her clear blue eyes. Joe Miller was in back of her—a tall, rangy, sandy-haired man with a big voice and the kind of a handshake that makes your fingers tingle. The four kids scrambled around Ann. They were a lively, bright-eyed bunch just as Ann had described them.

Everybody laughed and talked at the same time. Ann kissed them all, and then took three-year-old Jeanie in her arms. You could see that Mrs. Miller was so happy to have Ann home for Christmas that she had all she could do to keep from crying. As for Joe, he didn't say much, but the way he looked at Ann was enough to show how proud he was of her.

After things had quieted down and the welcome was over, I began to sense a certain tenseness in the air. And not until we were seated at the supper table, and Joe had shifted the conversation from Christmas and turkey for dinner to college, did I get an idea of what was worrying him.

"So you're singing all the time now with that dance band?" Joe said to Ann.

I knew then what was troubling them. Ann must have told them in her letters about her future plans, and her folks didn't exactly like them. The way he spoke I knew he figured that they shouldn't stand in her way if going on the road with Eddie Fowler's band was the wise thing to do. For all they knew, perhaps it was Ann's big chance, a first step to success.

But almost before Ann could answer Joe's question, Mrs. Miller changed the subject.

* * * * *

The meal over, the three boys began to fret about the storm making them miss the Christmas Eve program at the church. Joe wandered to a window and stood there with his big hands deep in his pockets. Presently he turned, grinning broadly.

"Why," he said, "I guess we don't let a little snow like this keep us home. You boys want to help me put clean hay in the wagon and hook up the horses? They haven't felt a harness in months—be plenty frisky tonight."

The boys yelled like Indians, and made a rush for their coats. Jeanie excitedly ran around in circles tagging after one and then another.

Kate had never ridden in a lumber wagon before, and I hadn't been in one for years. That was one of the best trips I ever had—with the children laughing and talking around us. It rolled back the years, and I began to feel as I had long ago when our family went to the Christmas service—happy and believing in all good things.

It wasn't long before we reached the little country church. Not a very large church as churches go. A single long room heated by a big cherry-red stove. Plain pine pews, and clear glass windows made for letting in the light. Or for letting it shine out, as the case might be. A great evergreen tree up front, decorated with strings of red berries and popcorn and colored paper chains—all the things that kids love to make with their own hands. And an old wheezy organ almost hidden under green boughs and sprigs of holly.

* * * * *

The storm had kept a good many people away, and I saw quite a few empty seats as I glanced around. And then I saw Stanley Arnold, as fair haired and clean looking as I remembered him from my brief contact with him in my choir. But Stanley didn't see me. Not at first, anyway. He had eyes only for Ann Stafford at the moment.

I'm not sure whether it was Mrs. Miller or Joe who suggested that I play the organ for them. Anyway, the next thing I knew I was up in front of these people, asking them what they wanted to hear.

Some of it, I didn't do very well, for I hadn't played it for a long time; but they liked it just the same. And right in the middle of my version of "Jingle Bells," I had an inspiration.

I stopped, grinned, and said, "There are two young people here who used to sing together in my choir at Ames. Ann Stafford and Stanley Arnold. Perhaps they'd come up here and help me."

That struck the crowd just right. Someone pushed Stanley to his feet. He looked doubtfully at Ann, and she looked at him, and they both smiled a bit shyly. But she didn't make a move to leave her seat, and Stanley sat down.

* * * * *

I thought that was the end of it. And it would have been if it hadn't been for Kate. What a wonderful woman! She caught Ann by the hand and pulled her to her feet and out into the aisle. Stanley came right over to Ann and, almost before they knew it, they were on their way to the organ.

They stood close together and looked as happy as any two I've ever seen. The worry and uncertainty were gone. If Ann had been confused before, certainly there was no doubt now in the tremulous smile she gave Stanley.

They sang the old songs. The songs they both understood and loved, and they sang from their hearts.

Their last number, "Silent Night, Holy Night," ended amid a reverent and unbroken hush; and they stepped to an empty front pew and sat down together. Ann's eyes were misty, but I doubt she even knew it as she smiled at Stanley.

Ann didn't ride home with us that night in the wagon. Stanley brought her after he'd taken his father and mother home. It was quite late, but I was still awake when they came into the big square house, laughing merrily.

* * * * *

Christmas Day, after the roads were cleared and Kate and I were about to drive on to Council Bluffs for the delayed organ recital, I said to Ann: "Well, we'll stop by tomorrow and pick you up."

She smiled and shook her head. "Thank you, but I'm staying home until vacation is over."

I didn't want to let it end there. But Kate shooed me out of there and into the car without giving me a chance to say another word.

Two weeks later at the end of Christmas vacation, Ann returned to Ames. After the first choir rehearsal, she came up to me and said, "If you haven't hired anyone else to be your librarian next semester, I'd like to keep the job."

"Fine!" I said. "But what about the Madcats?"

"Eddie'll have to find another singer," she answered, her eyes bright and happy. "I'm going to finish this year at Iowa State. Then teach a year or so and—well, Stan and I haven't made quite all our plans yet."

———————————

Frank Bennett wrote for popular magazines during the second half of the twentieth century.

Grandma Thomas's Three Christmas Trees

Jean Jeffrey Gietzen

All year long, Grandma Thomas saved her pennies so that, at the end of the year, she'd have enough money to buy a Christmas tree.

Well, one year, she had enough pennies saved up to buy three Christmas trees. Two of them found homes, but the third—well, therein hangs this story.

* * * * *

It was one of my grandmother's traditions to buy her Christmas tree with pennies saved throughout the year. Along about the feast of the Epiphany, Grandma Thomas would rinse out a big jug, stuff it with newspaper to collect the extra moisture, and, when she felt the jug was ready, out would come the newspaper and *clink-clink-clink* in would go the first of many pennies.

"Probably won't have enough this year," she'd always sigh as she dropped the pennies in, "but I'll start the jug anyway. You just never know what tomorrow will bring."

Grandma Thomas's penny jug never failed to produce enough money to purchase the best tree on the lot. One year, she even had enough money to buy not one, not two, but *three* Christmas trees.

"Well, now, Jeanie," Grandma Thomas chuckled, "here's my tree and here's a tree for—*hmm*—let me think." Grandma Thomas looked the tree over from top to bottom, giving it what I knew was her best think. Finally, she said, "Well, here's a tree for, well you just never know who. We'll see what tomorrow will bring."

I suggested that rather than waiting for tomorrow, we give the third tree to the orphanage, but my grandmother reminded me that the Knights of Columbus always had that honor. She tapped the tree on the ground a few times, mentioning and then dismissing names of our town's neediest families.

"No, no," she said, dismissing a name, "they won't take charity." Another dismissal was accompanied by, "Heard they were moving on."

No matter how many thinks we thought, neither my grandmother nor I could decide what to do with the extra tree. So we loaded all three of them into the trunk of Grandma's old Chevy and drove away from the lot still making suggestions to one another.

"We'll just line them up out back of your house for a few days," Grandma Thomas said as we pulled into our driveway. "Now, Jeanie, help me fill the tubs with snow and we'll stand them up in a row and see which ones need a shave and a haircut before we take them into the house."

Our Christmas trees stood proudly in their tubs for the next few days, and when my father and mother finally agreed on where to put the tree that year, my brother and I wrestled

one tree from its tub and lugged it into the house. As we decorated the tree, we discussed the fate of the last of the trio.

"It will be *soo* lonely out there if it doesn't have a home," I whined.

"Trees don't have feelings," my brother Tom said. "You're such a baby all the time."

"Raymond," Grandma Thomas said, "surely you know someone who needs a tree and can't afford it. What about that family over on the west side, the one with all those children?"

"Why, Grace Thomas!" my father said. "Surely you don't mean the Lowensteins?"

"Oh, for the love of heaven," my grandmother blushed. "I must be having one of my memory attacks. Of course. They don't celebrate Christmas."

"Not celebrate Christmas!" I gasped. "How sad for all those children. They must be very poor."

My father assured me that, quite to the contrary, the Lowensteins were rich in the things that really mattered: strong family ties, a deep, ancient faith. And even though they did not have much money, my father said that they were rich beyond my wildest imagination.

"Ha!" snorted my brother. "That makes them close to millionaires."

* * * * *

Rather than try to defend myself, I began to imagine a way in which I could meet these Lowensteins and convert them in time to celebrate Christmas. We had been studying the spread of Christianity in school and I could see no reason why I couldn't continue the process right here in North Dakota.

On the very next day, I put my plan in action. I missed my afternoon radio shows, but the adventures of Jack Armstrong were nothing compared to the adventurous journey I would make to the west side. I debated about whether or not to take my coin purse with me. Hadn't someone mentioned that Mr. Lowenstein ran a bakery? But Sister Clara had said the disciples had taken neither purse nor satchel and I was determined to follow them as closely as possible.

My first foray into the west end of town began with great courage. I practiced my conversion speech all the way there. But by the time I stood in front of Eddie Lowenstein's Bakery and Delicatessen, my hunger pains routed my courage and I would have sold my soul for one of Eddie's bagels. Maybe the disciples had gone from town to town with no money, but I wondered how they had had the strength to convert anyone when their stomachs were rumbling.

My second foray was also a disaster. The bakery owner himself caught me gazing in his window and raised his arm to shoo me away. Another day, he moved swiftly to the door when he saw me coming, but before he could open it, I had fled to the doorway of H. Rand, the tailor. This conversion business was rougher than I had imagined it would be, but I was determined to stick it out. My motto was, "You just never know what tomorrow will bring."

When I didn't make it home from the west side of town for the trip to Grandma's house to put up her tree, and then refused to say where I had been, my parents grounded me un-

til Christmas Eve, two whole days away. From my bedroom window, I could see the last of the Christmas trees looking as forlorn as I felt in my upstairs bedroom. My conversion plans had all been for naught and now the extra tree would just go to waste. I flopped out on my bed, dragged my Big Chief pad out from under my pillow, and began to write a tragic story about a poor, lonely, forgotten Christmas tree.

* * * * *

Christmas Eve came at last and along with it came my freedom. My grandmother and I made plans to celebrate by stepping out for some last minute shopping. Grandma Thomas even promised me a special treat for taking my punishment like a real martyr. We stopped at Woolworth's for pipe cleaners for my father, popped in and out of several stores looking for stockings for my mother, and spent what seemed like hours in the bookstore looking for a good almanac for my brother. When it was finally "treat" time, I assumed Grandma Thomas and I would go to Nelson's Ice Cream Store for banana splits. Instead, Grandma Thomas pointed her Chevy in the opposite direction. Christmas lights and decorations spun past me in a blur as I realized we were headed for the west side of town.

When we pulled up in front of Eddie's Bakery and Delicatessen, my heart rose in my throat as I asked, "Grandma, what are we doing here?"

"What have you been doing for several days running, young lady?" my grandmother asked with just a hint of scolding to her voice. "Eddie Lowenstein has been frantic with worry about the little girl who presses her nose up to the window so often that it's almost dented. He's asked everyone in town who the little girl is who runs away every time he beckons her inside. He's been going crazy trying to figure out why she hides at the tailor's just when he opens the door to the bakery. Someone finally told him they thought you were Ray Jeffrey's daughter. C'mon, now. You had better 'fess up."

"Oh, Grandma," I said with a long sigh. "I just wanted to convert Mr. Lowenstein by Christmas so we could give him the poor, lonely tree. I wanted to be a disciple and spread Christianity all over the world. But I don't have any courage at all and maybe I am a baby, just like Tommy says."

Grandma Thomas gave me a long hug and when she was done wiping the tears off of my face, she suggested we go into the bakery for a treat and meet Mr. Lowenstein.

Although I was embarrassed to do so, I followed my grandmother into the bakery. Grandma Thomas introduced herself, bought half a dozen bagels, and then said, "Mr. Lowenstein, this is Jeanie, the little girl who has had you so mystified."

Mr. Lowenstein squatted down to get a better look at me. "So," he said gently. "So you are not a lonely little street urchin after all. But why did you not come in when I beckoned? And why did you run from me? Why did you hover around my shop like a hummingbird?"

"I am not lonely, Mr. Lowenstein," I said, "but I have an extra Christmas tree in the backyard and it is lonely. I wanted you to become a Christian so I could give you my tree and it would be happy."

Mr. Lowenstein reached into his back pocket and pulled out a handkerchief. When he had finished blowing his nose and wiping his eyes, he said, "Such courage I have not seen. Such kindness to a little tree. Your goodness and kindness will be rewarded."

Mr. Lowenstein went behind the counter and began filling up a little sack.

"In this bag," he called out as he worked, "in this bag, I am putting some suet, some bread crumbs, and some of my plumpest raisins. When you go home tonight you must sprinkle this all around your tree. And in the morning, I will still be Mr. Lowenstein, your friend, the Jewish baker. In the morning you will still be Jeanie, a courageous friend of Jesus. But your tree, Jeanie, your lonely Christmas tree—ah! Your tree will be converted!" Mr. Lowenstein placed the bag triumphantly on top of Grandma's bagel bag and ushered us out the door.

I did exactly as Mr. Lowenstein had instructed me, and on Christmas morning, I saw every bird in the world fluttering around my proud, happy Christmas tree. No tree ever looked more beautiful, no carols sung could ever match the songs the birds sang as they announced their enjoyment of Mr. Lowenstein's gifts. Even though I had given up, a conversion had indeed taken place right here in the backyard of a little town in North Dakota.

When the feast of the Epiphany came around again, Grandma Thomas and I eagerly got the penny jug ready and hoped that we would have enough that year for three trees—one for Grandma Thomas, one for our family, and one for—well, you just can't tell. After all, you never know what tomorrow will bring.

Jean Jeffrey Gietzen writes for popular and inspirational magazines from her home in Milwaukee, Wisconsin.

An Exchange of Gifts

Diane Rayner

Marty was trying to give—in secret. A good thing, his mother reasoned. But what she couldn't figure out is why God would punish her son for that act with an electric fence.

* * * * *

I grew up believing that Christmas was a time when strange and wonderful things happened, when wise and royal visitors came riding, when at midnight the barnyard animals talked to one another, and in the light of a fabulous star, God came down to us as a Child. Christmas to me has always been a time of enchantment, and never more so than the year my son, Marty, was eight.

That was the year my children and I moved into a cozy trailer home in a forested area just outside of Redmond, Washington. As the holiday approached, our spirits were light, not to be dampened even by the winter rains that swept down Puget Sound to douse our home and make our floors muddy.

Throughout that December, Marty had been the most spirited and busiest of us all. He was my youngest—a cheerful boy, blond and playful, with a quaint habit of looking up at you and cocking his head like a puppy when you spoke to him. The reason for this was that Marty was deaf in his left

ear, but it was a condition he never complained about.

For weeks I had been watching Marty. I knew something was going on that he was not telling me about. I saw how eagerly he made his bed, took out the trash, and carefully set the table and helped Rick and Pam prepare dinner before I got home from work. I saw how he silently collected his allowance and tucked it away, not spending a cent of it. I had no idea what all this quiet activity was about, but I suspected it had something to do with Kenny.

Kenny was Marty's friend, and ever since they had found each other in the springtime, they were seldom apart. If you called to one, you got them both. Their world was in the meadow—a horse pasture broken by a small winding stream—where they caught frogs and snakes, searched for arrowheads or hidden treasure, or spent afternoons feeding peanuts to squirrels.

Times were hard for our family, and we had to do some scrimping to get by. Thanks to my job as a meat wrapper and a lot of ingenuity, we managed to have elegance on a shoestring. But not Kenny's family. They were desperately poor, and his mother was struggling to feed and clothe her two children. They were a good, solid family, but Kenny's mom was a proud woman, and she had strict rules.

How we worked, as we did each year, to make our home festive for the holiday! Ours was a handcrafted Christmas of gifts hidden away and ornaments strung about the place.

Marty and Kenny sometimes sat still at the table long enough to help make cornucopias or weave baskets for the tree; but then one whispered to the other, and they were out the door in a flash, and sliding cautiously under the electric fence into the horse pasture that separated our home from Kenny's.

One night shortly before Christmas, when my hands were deep in *pebernødder* dough, shaping nutlike Danish cookies heavily spiced with cinnamon, Marty came to me and said in a tone mixed with pleasure and pride, "Mom, I've bought Kenny a Christmas present. Want to see it?" *So that's what he's been up to,* I thought. "It's something he's wanted for a long, long time, Mom."

After carefully wiping his hands on a dishtowel, he pulled a small box from his pocket. Lifting the lid, I gazed at the pocket compass that my son had been saving all those allowances to buy.

"It's a lovely gift, Martin," I said, but even as I spoke, a disturbing thought came to mind. I knew how Kenny's mother felt about their poverty. They could barely afford to exchange gifts among themselves and giving presents to others was out of the question. I was sure she would not permit her son to receive something he could not return in kind.

Gently, carefully, I talked over the problem with Marty. He understood what I was saying.

"I know, Mom, I know, but what if it was a *secret*? What if they never found out *who* gave it?"

I didn't know how to answer him.

The day before Christmas was rainy, cold, and gray. The three kids and I all but fell over one another as we elbowed our way about our home putting finishing touches on secret Christmas gifts and preparing for family and friends who would drop by.

Night settled in. The rain continued. I looked out the window over the sink and felt an odd sadness. How mundane the rain seemed for a Christmas Eve. Would wise men come on such a night? I doubted it. It seemed to me that strange and wonderful things happened only on clear nights, nights when one could at least see a star in the heavens.

I turned from the window, and as I checked on the ham and *lefse* bread warming in the oven, I saw Marty slip out the door. He wore his coat over his pajamas, and he clutched a tiny, colorfully wrapped box.

Down through the soggy pasture he went, then under the electric fence and across the yard to Kenny's house. Up the steps on tiptoe, shoes squishing; open the screen door just a crack; place the gift on the doorstep; then take a deep breath, reach for the doorbell, and press on it *hard*.

Quickly Marty turned and ran down the steps and across the yard in a wild race to get away unnoticed. Then, suddenly, he banged into the electric fence.

The shock sent him reeling. He lay stunned on the wet ground. His body tingled, and he gasped for breath. Then slowly, weakly, confused and frightened, he began the grueling trip back home.

"Marty," I cried as he stumbled through the door, "what happened?" His lower lip quivered, his eyes brimmed.

"I forgot about the fence, and it knocked me down!"

I hugged his muddy body to me. He was still dazed, and there was a red mark beginning to blister on his face from his mouth to his ear. Quickly I treated the blister and, with a warm cup of cocoa soothing him, Marty's bright spirits returned. I tucked him into bed and just before he fell asleep he looked up at me and said, "Mom, Kenny didn't see me. I'm sure he didn't see me."

That Christmas Eve I went to bed unhappy and puzzled. It seemed such a cruel thing to happen to a little boy who was doing what the Lord wants us all to do, giving to others, and giving in secret at that. I did not sleep well that night.

Somewhere deep inside I think I must have been feeling the disappointment that Christmas had come and it had been just an ordinary, problem-filled night, no mysterious enchantment at all.

But I was wrong. By morning the rain stopped and the sun shone. The streak on Marty's face was red, but I could tell that the burn was not serious. We opened our presents, and soon, not unexpectedly, Kenny was knocking on the door, eager to show Marty his new compass and tell about the mystery of its arrival. It was plain that Kenny didn't suspect Marty at all, and while the two of them talked, Marty just smiled and smiled.

Then I noticed that while the two boys were comparing their Christmases, nodding and gesturing and chattering away, Marty was not cocking his head when Kenny was talking. Marty seemed to be listening with his deaf ear. Weeks later, a report came from the school nurse, verifying what Marty and I already knew, "Marty now has complete hearing in both ears."

How Marty regained his hearing, and still has it, remains a mystery. Doctors suspect that the shock from the electric fence was somehow responsible. Perhaps so. Whatever the reason, I am thankful to God for the good exchange of gifts that was made that night.

So you see, strange and wonderful things still happen on the night of our Lord's birth. And one does not have to have a clear night, either, to follow a fabulous star.

Diane Rayner wrote for popular and inspirational magazines during the second half of the twentieth century.

Empty Heart

Claire Jones

*"Miss Martha"—where had all the years gone? Where
had her youth, her life, gone? She was growing old before
her time.*

*And then . . . a slip on the icy pavement and excruciating pain. Now she'd not even be able to go buy a Christmas
tree.*

Little did she know. . . .

* * * * *

It was nearly four o'clock and already growing dark when
Martha Orcutt locked the door of the Springdale Memorial Library and stepped into the icy east wind.

She needn't have kept the library open past noon on
Christmas Eve. Only one or two people had come in that
morning, and surely no one would be interested in spending
the afternoon before Christmas in the library. But she had
had last week's shipment of new books to catalog; and it had
been a good time to work, with no interruptions.

Her mother wouldn't begin to worry about her until dark,
but the old lady was lonely and Martha's coming was the only
event of her day.

Martha sighed, pulled her coat about her tightly, and began the cold walk home. The evening stretched ahead of her,

long and lonely. Her mother would go to bed soon after supper, leaving Martha to spend the dreary hours alone in the
big, barnlike house.

She had brought two of the new books from the library
with her. She would spend the evening reading, as she always
did, would listen to the ten o'clock news on the radio, and
then go to bed. Not a very exciting routine on any night, and
certainly not satisfying on Christmas Eve.

Mr. Webster, who had the insurance agency in the next
block, passed her, his pleasant round face red with cold.

"Evening, Miss Martha," he said as he passed.

Martha smiled back, but there was a tightness in her
throat. Miss Martha! It was Springdale's way of speaking of all
its maiden ladies—Miss Hannah, who had first grade through
three generations; Miss Amy, who had been making dresses
for Springdale women for nearly fifty years.

When had it happened to *her*? When had she stopped
being Judge Orcutt's little girl? When had she stopped being Miss Orcutt, home for the summer vacation from college? Miss Orcutt, postponing her plans for graduate work in
the city to help care for her father in his last, long illness?
The time had gone so quickly. Where had the dreams gone?
Where had the hopes vanished?

She smiled mirthlessly as she plodded through the gloomy
afternoon. She could guess how she looked to Mr. Webster, to
the rest of Springdale—brown hair, brown eyes, pale skin—
undistinguished, faded a little perhaps. But surely not in a
category with the Miss Hannahs and the Miss Amys of the
town.

The wind struck her an icy blow, and the smile faded.
"Face it," she said to herself. "You have nothing to look for-

ward to. You are tied to Springdale, tied to the old Orcutt house, to the tattered remnants of the Orcutt pride."

She had been in her first year of graduate study when her father had taken ill. She had come home, just temporarily, but the illness had been a long one. Then, after her father's death, her mother had been ill a long time. She was better now, able to care for herself, but badly crippled with arthritis and certainly in no condition to be left alone.

Martha had lost the dream of going back to school, and she was not qualified to work anywhere but in Springdale. The library was a good one, but small, and the salary was meager. Springdale didn't mind that she had no degree in library science. With her mother's small income from her father's estate and Martha's modest contribution, they managed—barely.

They ought to sell the house. Heating bills were enormous in the winter months. Upkeep and essential repairs kept their tight budget depleted. Insurance, taxes, medicines for her mother—all were never ending worries.

But her mother wouldn't hear of leaving the Orcutt house. "We've always managed. We always will. The Orcutts can take care of themselves."

The Orcutt pride! So they had gone on, the two of them, living in the big, slightly shabby house, that had once been a showplace in Springdale. More and more each year, they lived to themselves.

Her mother had been a shut-in for so long, few people came to see her anymore. Many of her old friends were dead. Others, not well themselves, came infrequently.

The Orcutts took no interest in civic affairs. They almost never went to church. "We can't give anymore, and we won't go," her mother said. "The Orcutts pay their way."

Martha's contemporaries had moved away or were comfortably and busily occupied with growing families. She was rarely included in social activities. She couldn't reciprocate with luncheons or dinners or rides, and she had turned down invitations until they had gradually ceased.

It was almost dark when Martha came to the corner of River Street, where the Orcutt house stood proudly in the middle of the block. She was chilled through and bitterly tired. Tears of self-pity pricked at her eyes.

The house next door was ablaze with lights. There was a cutout sleigh and reindeer in the yard. Joe Roselli had fastened a huge, lighted star to the gable of his house. Wreaths adorned every window. A Christmas tree sparkled in the living room window. The Roselli family was making a great deal of Christmas. They always did.

The door of the house burst open and Gina and Tony, ten-year-old twins who were the liveliest members of the Roselli brood, came out. Music and laughter spilled out of the door behind them.

Gina caught sight of Martha and waved shyly. "Hi, Miss Martha," she said. "We came out to see how the reindeer look, now it's dark."

Martha waved back. She didn't answer. "Miss Martha" again. The tears that had been threatening spilled over and ran down her cheeks. She brushed them away impatiently.

She rarely cried. Most of the time she accepted things as they were—not happily—but with the resignation of long submission. But this was Christmas Eve! A time for dreams, for hope. *Even for me*, she thought.

Her mother was sitting close to the fire in the living room. She looked little and frail and tired. Martha forced a smile.

She bent down and kissed her mother lightly.

"Who was that outside, Martha?" Her mother was lonely, Martha knew, but she would never admit it.

Martha plumped up the pillows at her mother's back. "I was talking to Gina and Tony," she said. "Have you seen their house, Mother? Wreaths, and stars and even a sleigh and reindeer."

Her mother sniffed. "I'm not surprised. Joe Roselli ought to have his house painted instead of spending all that money on foolishness," she added, her mouth tight with disapproval. "I don't know what this neighborhood is coming to. In your grandfather's day, only the old families of Springdale lived on this street."

"Joe isn't exactly a newcomer, Mother," Martha protested. For years his mother and father had owned the small grocery store that was now his. Joe had been born in Springdale.

"They have such fun together, Mother," Martha said. "And it couldn't have been easy for Mr. Roselli, taking care of five children alone all these years since his wife's death. They have tried to be kind to us."

Her mother sniffed again. "We don't need favors."

Martha sighed. There was no use arguing with her mother. But the Rosellis had tried to be kind. The first few years they had lived in the house next door, big, smiling Joe Roselli had tried to help the women in many ways.

He shoveled snow for them in winter, offered to paint the fence, sent Nick, his oldest, to carry packages for Martha. But Martha, unable to pay for the services, had refused so many times that finally Joe had stopped offering.

Nick had mowed the yard for several summers, but when even that expense had become more than they could afford, Martha had stopped it. She refused firmly when Joe said Nick would be glad to do it for nothing. "Because we are neighbors," Mr. Roselli had said.

But the Orcutts didn't accept favors. Martha got up early on summer mornings to mow the lawn herself before going to the library.

Martha moved to the window to look again at the brightly lighted house next door. It looked festive in the frosty afternoon. By contrast, the Orcutt's house was cheerless and dark—not a wreath, not a colored light, not even a tree in the big, neat living room. Martha made a sudden decision.

"If you'll be all right for a little while, Mother, I'm going over to the avenue for a minute. Dinner won't take a minute tonight, and it's not five."

"What in the world do you want to go out for? You got enough groceries yesterday to last us a week."

"I know," Martha said. "I'm not going to get groceries." She added a little defiantly, "I'm going to get a Christmas tree."

Her mother frowned. "Be sensible, Martha! Christmas trees are for children. We surely don't need to spend money for such foolishness. I can't imagine why you'd want to go out again on a night like this—for a Christmas tree!"

Martha wanted to cry out, *Because I want to feel a part of Christmas; because I want a little of its magic, even if it is only a tinseled tree.* But she only said, stubbornly, "If you think you'll be all right."

"Of course I'll be all right," her mother said crossly. "But I do think it's foolish."

Martha escaped quickly, before her mother could change her mind and call her back. It was quite dark now. The wind was sharper. The trees crackled beneath their coating of ice.

She bent her head against the wind and started quickly down the street. She was opposite the walk leading to the Roselli's brightly lighted front door when her foot found a patch of ice on the sidewalk, and she slipped. She fell heavily, a tearing pain in her ankle.

She lay stunned for a moment, waves of pain licking up the sides of her leg. Cautiously she tried to get to her feet. Her ankle gave way; and she sank to the ground again, waves of nausea sweeping over her.

She looked back at the Orcutt house. It looked frighteningly far away. She couldn't get back by herself. If only the ankle were not broken!

Her mother had been right. She had been foolish to go out again. For a Christmas tree! Now they would have a fine Christmas! And what would they do if she were unable to walk for weeks? She choked back a sob of vexation and pain.

The door of the Roselli house opened, and Nick came out into the yard, a lightbulb in his hand. "I'll fix it, Dad," he called back over his shoulder.

Then he saw Martha, huddled at the end of the walk. He came closer and said in astonishment, "Miss Martha!" He knelt beside her and called, "Dad! Dad! It's Miss Martha. She's hurt!"

Joe Roselli hurried out of the house, followed by the rest of the family—Angela, the oldest girl; Tony and Gina; little Anna, the youngest. They crowded around Martha until their father pushed them back. His strong arm went about Martha.

"Are you badly hurt?" he asked.

"I—I don't know," she said. "I've twisted my ankle—if I can just get home and call Dr. Franklin."

Joe picked her up in his arms as though she were one of the children and carried her into the house, the youngsters—big eyed and excited—following. He put her on the couch.

He took her ankle in his hands, his fingers surprisingly gentle, and manipulated it a little.

"A sprain, I think," he said, as she winced in pain. "But we had better be sure. Nick, call Dr. Franklin. Angela, bring a glass of water and then take the twins and Anna and go to the kitchen."

The children dispersed, and Martha lay back against the couch. "I don't want to be any trouble," she said. "I'll just go on home."

"We'll wait and see what the doctor says," Joe said. "I'm going to get you a blanket."

He disappeared into the back regions of the house. There was nothing for Martha to do but wait.

In spite of her distraught condition, she was impressed with the warmth and cheer of the Roselli living room. The huge tree sparkled in the corner, lighted candles glowing on the mantel. There were books and magazines, plants and flowers. A plump cat curled in a furry ball on the hearth. The aroma of turkey and cooling pumpkin pies seeped in from the kitchen. It was a friendly room, warm with life and with love.

Martha realized suddenly, with an odd sense of shame, that she had never been in this house in all the years the Rosellis had been her neighbors.

When Dr. Franklin arrived, bustling and apple-cheeked from the cold, he confirmed Joe's diagnosis.

"A bad sprain," he said. "Stay off it a few days, and then use it as you can."

"Have you as good as new in a couple of weeks." He knew Martha's situation. He had been their doctor for years. "Can you manage? With your mother, I mean?"

Joe answered before she could. "We'll take care of her, Dr.

Franklin. Angela can help out over there until Miss Orcutt can get about again. And Nick and Tony are good at doing chores. She'll be fine."

Before Martha could protest, he was at the door with Dr. Franklin, wishing him a Merry Christmas, and closing the door behind him.

The children, their eyes bright with curiosity, had edged back into the room again.

"Is she all right, Daddy?" Anna asked.

Joe smiled. "She's fine. Now I'll tell you what we are going to do. Miss Orcutt is going to spend Christmas Eve here with us. Angela, you and I are going next door to bring Mrs. Orcutt too. They are going to have dinner with us."

He smiled at Martha. "I carried you in; I can surely carry your mother. Gina, put two more places at the table, quickly."

"No!" Martha said, "No, we can't do that!"

"But why not? Have you other plans for tonight?"

Martha flushed. He would know they never had other plans. She said stiffly, "We can't intrude on your Christmas celebration. We really can't. We wouldn't think of it."

"Nonsense," Joe's smile dimmed a little. "There is always room for more at Christmastime."

Martha shook her head firmly. "I'm sorry. It's kind of you. But we just couldn't do that. And Angela and the boys needn't spoil their holiday by worrying about us. Mother and I can manage. We don't need—"

She stopped in confusion, leaving the sentence unfinished.

"I see," said Joe slowly. "You don't need help from us. That's what you were going to say, wasn't it? You don't need help. You don't want help." His eyes were cold now.

He turned to the children who were listening quietly, sensing but not quite understanding the tension in the room. "Go into the kitchen," he said quietly. "All of you. And close the door. I want to talk to Miss Orcutt alone for a few minutes."

They went obediently, closing the door behind them as they left the room.

"I'm sorry, Mr. Roselli," she said. "I don't mean to offend you. I appreciate—"

Joe interrupted her. "All right," he said, and his voice was harsh. "Get up now and go on home."

Martha drew in her breath in shock and surprise. Her cheeks were flaming. She made an effort to get up, but the pain in her ankle forced her to sit down again.

Joe watched her, his face impassive. He said in the same cold voice, "Go on, now!"

In spite of all her efforts to control them, tears were swimming in her eyes. She made another effort to rise. Pride kept her head high, but in spite of herself she stumbled, and had to grab the back of an armchair to keep from falling.

The quiet voice was unyielding. "Go on home, Miss Orcutt."

Humiliatingly, her tears broke loose. Angry and helpless, she had to say, "I can't. I can't go by myself."

"Then ask me to help you," he said. "Ask me to help you."

"Please—" she was sobbing uncontrollably now.

"Ask me!" His voice was quiet and inexorable.

She reached out her hand, "Help me, please help me."

He caught her as she stumbled and helped her back to the couch. She turned her head away from him and cried helplessly, hurt and humiliation flooding over her.

"I'm sorry, Martha," he said, and now his voice was gentle. "But I had to make you see that not one of us can go through life alone. We all need others. We all have to ask for help. We all need to give help. But you—you give nothing, and you accept nothing from anyone."

Stung afresh, Martha cried out, "You have no right. I look after Mother. But I won't take where I have nothing to give. The Orcutts don't take favors. We—"

Joe shook his head. "Oh Martha, Martha. The Orcutts are people. And people must give and people must take, or they are dead."

He turned her around to face him. "Your devotion to your mother is fine, but not enough. Everyone has something to give. When I moved into this house six years ago, my oldest child was nine, my youngest three. They were motherless. I needed help then, advice and counsel and understanding from someone who cared.

"Neither you nor your mother even came to see if there were needs that you could meet. Perhaps, even worse, you refused to let me and my children serve you for nothing but the pleasure of service, and so withheld from us the greatest gift of all."

His eyes looked deep into hers. "Martha, it is Christmas. A time for giving. A time for receiving. Don't you waste another year!"

Martha looked into his eyes. The words of defense and anger she wanted to say died on her lips. He was right! From the moment he had forced the cry of need from her, she had known why her life had been so empty, so meaningless. How could she have hoped to feel a part of Christmas, alone—shut away from the needs, the help of others?

Then she was crying again, warm tears that came from the hidden springs of her heart.

Joe reached out and patted her arm as though she were Anna. When at last the tears stopped, she sat up and asked, as Anna might have asked, "It isn't too late for me, is it? Oh, it isn't too late now?"

He smiled, "No," he said gently. "It is never too late. And many things may come into the heart at Christmas, if we will make room for them."

They sat quietly in the warmth of the softly lighted room for a moment. Then Angela called timidly but hopefully from the kitchen.

"Everything's nearly ready, Daddy. And Nick says that he is awfully hungry."

Joe stood up. He laughed his hearty, big laugh. "We're hungry too. Let Gina dish up; you come with me, Angela."

He smiled at Martha. "We'll get your mother."

Martha smiled back. Joe could manage her mother. She was suddenly sure that he could.

"All right," she said. "And thank you. *Thank you.*"

At the door to the hall, he turned, "Merry Christmas, Martha," he said with feeling.

"Merry Christmas—Joe." A surge of warmth, of happiness swept over her. She was smiling radiantly as she watched him go.

Claire Jones wrote for popular and inspirational magazines early in the twentieth century.

The Rugged Road

Margaret E. Sangster Jr.

The Youngest Thief had never known what it felt like not to think and act like a thief—until that night!

* * * * *

The camel tracks made a path, clear cut and white, across the sands of the desert. The Youngest Thief, reining in his horse, was amazed at the depth, the clean definition of them.

"But the caravan—it must have been heavily laden!" he said slowly, and there was a note of regret, tinged with a grudging sort of respect, in his voice.

The Chief of the band was not listening. He was not even looking at the marks that wandered off toward the horizon line. He was staring—and there was an almost apprehensive expression on his lean, hawklike face—into the height of heavens. Heavens that hung like a deep blue tent above the desert—wide and star-flecked and wonderful.

"There is a strange light," he said at last, "almost an unearthly light—coming from above. Perhaps it is an omen. Perhaps it is just as well that we were too late!"

The Youngest Thief shrugged impatient shoulders. Because he was the youngest—and therefore the favored one—he dared shrug his shoulders!

"Certainly," he urged, "you will not give up the chase? The camel tracks are not old. And horses are swifter than these—" he laughed lightly, "these beasts of burden. With any sort of luck we could overtake the caravan before it reaches a town. And when we do—"

His slim, brown hand, twitching ever so slightly, reached in the direction of the long, curving knife that was twisted into the heavy silk of his girdle.

For a moment the Chief of the band was silent. And then, "And yet the light from above, it worries me," he said. "The tracks of the camels lie in the very direction that it points. Almost it might be that the light was guiding the caravan!"

The Youngest Thief laughed. "So—" he taunted boyishly, "so—the shine of a single star has worried my master? Is it not possible that we shall be glad of its guiding—we also."

But the Chief was ignoring the laughter, the youthful arrogance. "I had not realized, until you spoke," he said—and something akin to fear lay in his voice—"that the radiance was born of a single star! I had not—realized."

And it was true. As they spurred their steeds onward, even the Youngest Thief felt a curious sense of interest. For the light from above seemed momentarily to grow stronger, more sensitively beautiful. It bathed the desert in a calm glory—it drew the camel tracks, like some intangible magnet, toward the far friendliness of a town that waited upon the fringe of the sands. It lay like a gentle prayer across the tense, unresponsive faces of the men who followed the way that the caravan had taken.

Cruel faces they were—these! The silent, intent faces of men born to thievery, bred to the black arts of ruin and ravage and murder. Nomads—spawn of a trackless, pitiless, relentless country. Wanderers who lived by their cunning, their strength.

Perhaps it is, after all, environment that shapes—or, at least, colors—the soul. When one lives close to the fragrance of flowers, when one hears the ripple of water and the song of birds, one's heart may be attuned to the softer things of life. But in a place of sandstorms, of blinding suns, of death from hunger and from thirst, well . . .

Nomads they were. And plunderers. Wanderers and thieves by the laws of their land as well as by heredity. The Youngest Thief could remember, as a child, no tenderness. His fingers had been taught to creep quietly into a money bag, to touch a spear, at an age when the fingers of other little boys are groping softly across a mother's face.

His father had been a robber. So had his father's father. They, in turn, had served under the leadership of the present Chief's father and grandfather. And it was so with the other members of the band. They carried a price—each one of them—upon his head. And the price was a chain forged of the generations that had gone by.

Through the unexplainable quickening of the desert sense—a strange, almost magic wilderness telegraph—the band had learned of a rich caravan coming from a far country. Bearing gifts to a king. The king's name, to them, was as unknown as it was unimportant. It was only the treasure that mattered. They had girded on their weapons, had set forth into the shadows of the coming evening with the thought of a surprise attack in their minds. But somehow their calculations—usually so exact—had gone awry. And they had reached the appointed place too late. The caravan had passed.

There was, as the Youngest Thief had pointed out, a chance of overtaking the laden camels before the safety of a town could be gained. But if the town were entered, the hard riding and the crafty planning would go for naught. For, once inside the town, the caravan and the gifts that it bore were safe. No thief with a price upon his head dares enter beyond a city's wall!

Swiftly, riding in a long, slender column, the thieves swept across the desert. The leader rode first, as was his custom. But there was something curiously resigned in the slumping carriage of his broad shoulders. The Youngest Thief, riding ever so slightly behind his master, was aware of this subtle droop, and disturbed by it. Well he knew, as did the others of the band, that the strange quality of the starlight had disturbed their Chief. Indeed, the others of the band—superstitious men, all of them—were beginning to mutter. Even the Youngest Thief could scarcely help speculating. In all his life—a life spent in a land of amazing climactic conditions—he had never seen the like of the star that glowed, as a great lamp glows, above them. It was like riding through a cool daylight, a daylight that reached beyond a man's eyes—that dared penetrate into a man's soul!

They had ridden hard for hours. The flying hoofs of the horses were beating against the doors of midnight when the Youngest Thief sighted the caravan. Sighted it for the first time against the dreaming distance. With a cry he spurred his steed forward and caught at the flowing white robe of his leader.

"See," he cried, "see! We *will* overtake them!"

The Chief of the band turned eyes suddenly weary upon his young follower. His voice, when he spoke, came huskily.

"We will *not* overtake them," he said somberly, "for the town, which will be their haven, is but a short space beyond. A hundred yards farther, and you will glimpse the roofs of it.

We had best turn back. We have lost our chance."

Looking ahead, toward the caravan which wound like some animated toy over the white sand, the Youngest Thief acknowledged that his leader was right. Already he could glimpse a dark smudge upon the sky—in a few moments it would take on a definite outline. Yes, the caravan had very nearly gained the town. And it was still many miles away from them! Hot rage surged in the heart of the Youngest Thief.

"They have escaped us!" he rasped, and uttered a curse that rang like the clank of a saber upon the still air.

The leader of the band was laughing. His laughter had a slightly relieved note in it. "I, for one," he cried, and, wheeling his horse about, he spoke to his followers, "I, for one, am glad that the caravan has passed beyond all hope of capture. While this light—" his arm made a swinging gesture toward the sky, "while this light persists, we had best bide in peace."

The followers were cheering. They utterly agreed with their leader. Save only the Youngest Thief.

"But I," he grumbled, "am not so easily discouraged. I would still—"

The leader's laughter was growing in volume. "You would ride into the town, no

doubt," he chuckled, "eh, boy? And go through the town. *And follow to the very house of the king.*"

The Youngest Thief was flushing an ugly scarlet. After all, a prize—treasure—meant more to him than it did to the older men who had robbed many a rich caravan.

"Aye—that I would!" he retorted.

The leader of the band turned suddenly serious. "Then," he said, "then, my young warrior, suppose you do go on, alone. Perhaps, who knows, the caravan may be wending a way homeward erelong. With the return gifts of this king. You might gain for us information of value, if you choose to enter the town. With the information you will be welcome at our usual meeting place."

It was in the nature of a challenge. The Chief was not giving an order—he was making a suggestion. But although he knew the fate of a spy—especially of a robber spy—the Youngest Thief did not hesitate. He had never yet failed to stoop to a flung gauntlet.

"So be it," he said shortly.

And his horse, feeling the touch of emphatic spurs, leaped forward.

Leaping forward to follow the camel tracks that lay glimmering in a path of silver light.

* * * * *

As he came into the outskirts of the little town, the Youngest Thief dismounted from the tired horse that had carried him so swiftly. And, leading the beast by the bridle, he sauntered—as casually as he could—down the narrowest of the narrow streets. It was still night, for he had ridden hard. But despite the hour there was a stir about the place—an air of expectancy, an alert feeling. Perhaps—the Youngest Thief told himself—the town was aware of his presence. And then common sense assured him that he, alone, was scarcely important enough to keep a town awake and waiting.

It was still night. And yet it was not dark. The star that had made a path across the desert seemed to be concentrating its beams upon the town. It was almost as if the star were directly above the town!

The Youngest Thief shivered slightly. Perhaps, after all, it was an omen, as his leader had suggested. Certainly the starlight had led him—no, drawn him!—into the very heart of a city where a robber, if recognized, would be given a too-enthusiastic reception. Perhaps it was even a ruse of some sort. And yet—and yet—there was the caravan! And it had become his task to trace the caravan, to follow it.

The trail, even through the village byways, was plain. It led in the direction of the inn. Well, that was natural. The owners of the caravan would seek rest and refreshment after their long desert trip. The Youngest Thief, leading his horse, was almost glad when—only a stone's throw away—he glimpsed the town's small hostelry. The courtyard of it was strangely crowded, but—he figured to himself—the arrival of a large caravan would make a stir, of sorts, in such a place. Putting on a bold front, he advanced to the inn door. He, too, would come in the role of a desert-weary traveler. As such he addressed the host who stood on the threshold, nervously rubbing his hands together.

"I seek—rest," said the Youngest Thief.

The host threw his hands wide apart in a helpless gesture. "But there is no room at the inn," he answered.

The Youngest Thief, ever so slightly at a loss, hesitated. And then, "I may, at least, stable my horse?" he questioned.

But the host of the inn was speaking rapidly. "But the stable, too, is crowded," said the host.

Angrily, the Youngest Thief turned away. After all, what right had this small inn to be so overfull? As he wedged his way between the closely huddled people, he was muttering impatiently to himself.

Upon every side were evidences of the caravan that he had followed. Weary camels huddled into strange, unreal positions. Drowsy little donkeys. A fine Arabian horse or two. And servitors—many of them—dressed in a rich livery. One of these the Youngest Thief approached.

"Your master," he questioned, "he is a great man—yes? And . . . and he seeks a king, does he not? And he is bearing gifts?"

The servitor was unfastening a heavy pack. He spoke in a preoccupied manner. "My master," he said, "is a *very* great man. He is a prince of the East. He is called a wise man—he knows the meaning of all signs and symbols!"

The Youngest Thief persisted. "But the gifts that he is bearing—" he questioned, "the King that he has journeyed to find?"

The servitor was tired as well as preoccupied. He answered a shade crossly. "The star led us," answered the servitor. "It led us many leagues across plains and mountains and deserts. We met two other princes on the way—they made a part of our train. And then finally and together we came into this town. And the star pointed then our destination. To—" he laughed sarcastically, "to a stable! A fine place, one would say, in which to house a King!"

Amazement written upon his face, the Youngest Thief strolled away. It was strange, this whole proceeding. Who had ever heard of royalty finding refuge in a place of mangers and feed tubs and stalls? With a swift, catlike movement, he turned toward the stable—a squat, dingy building at the far end of the courtyard. And as he turned in that direction, he noticed that the light of the star lay in a warm circle all about the place.

There were shepherds, many of them, standing in the doorway of the stable. There were a number of retainers wearing the livery of the Eastern prince. Surveying them, the Youngest Thief deemed it unwise to try to force an entrance. But a sudden, consuming desire to see this King was burning in his breast. It was a curious feeling, almost like hunger. Only, not hunger of the body. He had, in a way, forgotten the real purpose of his visit. He had forgotten, almost, the gifts that he had hoped to steal.

There was a window in the wall of the stable, a narrow window set some distance apart from the door. To this window, the Youngest Thief made his way. It was with a throb of growing excitement that he laid his brown hands upon the sill; that he raised his eyes, and focused their glance upon the interior of the stable room.

* * * * *

His first feeling was one of amazement—touched with disappointment. What he had expected to see he scarcely knew, but certainly he had not expected to see such a poor place! Certainly he had not expected to see a prince, in the rich robes of ceremony, kneeling, while two other princes waited their turn before a woman—such a shabby woman!—with a

Baby in her arms. And yet—all at once he knew that his heart was beating heavily in his throat—that his hands, clenched upon the other sill of the window, were dry and hot.

The woman *was* shabby. But somehow there was a glow about her. Perhaps his gaze was still dazzled by the starshine, the Youngest Thief told himself. Or perhaps the glow was only the reflection of the tenderness that lay in the woman's eyes!

The prince, still kneeling, was opening a casket. It was filled with gold. Much gold. For one instant, the Youngest Thief was remembering his errand. And then he had again forgotten the treasure. For his mind, his soul, his whole body were groping forward—that he might better see the face of the Baby.

The face of the Baby! In after years the Youngest Thief tried, feature by feature, to remember it. And failed. For it was not the crumpled roseleaf of the Baby's mouth—the fluff that was the Baby's hair. It was not the blue—vague with the mystery of birth—of His eyes. They did not matter. Nor His groping, tiny hands. It was that thing—intangible, lovely—that the Baby suggested.

All at once the Youngest Thief, inarticulate and surprised, was thinking different thoughts from those he had ever dared to think. Of green fields and crystal streams and hilltops gay with early sunshine. All at once he was thinking of a life free and open—far from pettiness and horror and unfair dealings. He was thinking of a living earned decently and honestly—of men looking with unfurtive eyes into the eyes of their fellows. Suddenly—and from a full heart—he was praying. Unconsciously and wordlessly, to a God he did not recognize.

The prince in the stable room was kissing the hem of the mother's ragged garment. She was smiling, and her smile was like a misty pearl set in the silver of her pallid face. The Baby was drooping against her breast. The Baby was asleep.

Suddenly—like a waking from strength-giving slumber—the Youngest Thief tore himself away from the little window. Suddenly he was hurrying, his horse's bridle held tensely, through the courtyard. Suddenly—although he could not have explained it in coherent sentences—he knew the meaning of the radiant star. *And of life*.

As he hurried through the streets of the town, it seemed to him that he could hear—no, *sense*—the rhythm of far voices singing. Or was it only another, farther voice, speaking in his own heart?

It was not until he had gained the outskirts of the town, until he had mounted his horse, that complete realization came to him. It was only then that he knew that his mission had been quite forgotten. And that he would never return with a message to the band of desert thieves that waited, all too eagerly, for his coming.

* * * * *

Life is often a desert path that winds wearily across a lonely world. The Youngest Thief found it so. Unequipped for the practical ways of earning a living, he fared badly in his new role of honest man. His slim hands—agile and quick at the loosening of a money belt, deft in the bending of a bow or the throwing of a javelin—were unbelievably slow at the tasks that required infinitely less skill. A plow blistered his palms, and a saw—in his fingers—performed unbelievable atrocities upon a harmless piece of wood.

And then, too, the Youngest Thief found mental hazards—

uncrossable barriers that separated him from other men. He could not—without lying—tell of his past, of his people. And lying was outside his new code. With no background of any sort, it was almost impossible to make friends. And without friends, he found it difficult to gain his daily bread.

"I can ride," he would say, as he paused at the doorway of a man who owned many flocks. "I can fight. I know the conditions of desert life—"

And the herder, putting two and two together, would send him away and hire a man who played a reed flute while hapless sheep went wandering.

Many sorts of work the Youngest Thief tried. He was not proud; there was no labor too menial to interest him. But somehow he never seemed to last long in any one situation. Always the inevitable question would arise. At the table, while the laborers had their meat—in the cool of the evening, when they rested beneath the shade of trees.

"And, stranger," someone would say, "what did you do for a living ere you became one of us?"

And the Youngest Thief's silence would brand his yesterday as an ugly and shameful thing.

Days and months and years. They drifted across the Youngest Thief's soul. And each day, each month, each year, left its scar. These scars were torture to a wistful youth fast growing into a sad and disappointed man—a man beset with doubts and temptations.

For often, into that settlement, which was momentarily his home, there drifted tales of the band to which he had belonged—and its brutal prowess. A camel train, bearing the dead as a cargo, rather than merchandise, would enter by the desert road. And men would curse the nomad thieves who

had crept like a sandstorm upon defenseless folk. Men would curse while the Youngest Thief speculated as to each robber's share in the prize.

It would have been easy, so easy, to go back to the band! He had always been the leader's favorite. There would be a place, and forgiveness, awaiting him. And here, in the world of honest men, there was no place. And no forgiveness.

Oh, it would have been easy. But—with temptation would come the swift memory of a certain night when the light of a star made the whole earth beautiful and fair. When the face of a drowsy Baby had purified a youth's soul.

The first years were not the hardest years that the Youngest Thief faced. For then he was handsome and lithe and filled with courage. And when men failed to grant him the boon of toil, women smiled upon him and gave him meat to eat, and white bread from their tables. The first years were not hard—it was only when the grey had begun to show in his hair, when the jauntiness had gone from his spirit, that the Youngest Thief knew the dawn of despair. And yet—even when the clouds of gloom were heaviest, they could be dispelled by the remembered tenderness that lay in a mother's brooding eyes.

Often, as he fought his battle of faith, the Youngest Thief flexed his fingers to feel if they had lost their cunning. Without going back to the band, he might still ply the trade that had come to him through the training of generations. These honest folk were careless in the guarding of their many possessions—often a jewel or a shining coin could easily be removed from a stout, unwary hand. Once the Youngest Thief turned and ran from the sight of a matron who slept soundly beneath a cedar tree—with a ruby glistening redly upon her rhythmically rising breast. Ran with the dim memory of a

Child's pursed-up rosy mouth as his only guide.

As he grew older and more tired, the Youngest Thief became in villages a weary legend. A man homeless and nameless, who walked from place to place. Always tired, always unwanted, always alone. Sometimes the children of the place ran after him—sometimes stones were flung and dogs barked and old wives taunted. And the Youngest Thief—raising questioning eyes to a starless sky—would wonder at the meaning quite hidden from his heart.

Ten years, twenty years. Not rapid in their passing. As slow as the torment of a bad dream. Thirty years—untouched by the hand of friendship or understanding or kindliness. While, through the countryside—boiling over with want and discontent and crime—a rumor was spreading. The rumor of a Leader, who helped those who knew sickness of body and soul. Who gave happiness to those forgotten of men. But the Youngest Thief—young no longer—did not hear these rumors. Hungry, dirty, fearful—perhaps he would not have believed them had he heard!

The vision of the stable and the kneeling Price was far away in these days. The mother and the Baby were as faint—in his mind—as the perfume of a flower that has crumbled to dust. And yet the Youngest Thief still held to his purpose. And went openly from doorway to doorway, asking work, asking his meed of trust. Asking, always—and turning away from the expected answer with the tears of despair in his saddened eyes.

* * * * *

It couldn't go on—not forever. A man must eat. More weeks and months—springing again into years. And the Youngest Thief—hysterical with hunger—begging in a marketplace, with dirt upon the hands that he extended for alms.

If they had only listened! If the man with the beaded pouch, the bulging pouch that hung at his side, had only answered kindly! Perhaps it was the push of the man's arm, cloaked in silk, that brought the final forgetfulness to the tired brain of the Youngest Thief. Perhaps it was the sneering smile upon the man's round face that made the Youngest Thief stumble after him as he left the marketplace. It was not only the desire for food. Or—was it?

The man with the bulging pouch—the Youngest Thief could almost smell the money it contained—left the marketplace in the manner of one who is unhurried. The Youngest Thief, following him, saw everything about in a red haze through which the man's body ambled. The trees, the houses, reeled like grotesque figures in a crimson dance. The man with the beaded pouch had pushed him aside—and he was hungry. He had not eaten—the Youngest Thief hesitated mentally—in the sum of the days! He followed through thronged streets, his dirty fingers twitching at his sides.

It was at a crossroad that he overtook the man. That he laid a hand, utterly lacking in strength, upon the man's rich sleeve. And—

"I'm starving," he said. Just that.

The man was pudgy. With feet set wide apart in the road, he surveyed the Youngest Thief. And the word that he spoke—as one fat hand fondled the beaded pouch—was ugly.

Again the trees began to sway. Again the red haze was before the vision of the Youngest Thief. Like a man in a dream—perhaps he *was* a man in a dream—he stooped. And groping weakly in the dust of the road, felt, with his languid fingers, the smooth sides of a stone. It was heavy to lift—the stone—but it grew lighter as the pudgy man laughed contemptuously at the effort.

But the man stopped laughing when the stone crashed suddenly into his cruel and sneering face.

The world suddenly was clear again. The red haze had gone. Perhaps the screaming of many people had made the world turn back to its own color.

But the Youngest Thief, his hand on the beaded pouch of money, was staring past the faces of the gathering mob. He did not even feel the ungentle touch of a soldier's hand upon his lean shoulder.

He was trying, so hard, to remember . . .

* * * * *

And so they sentenced him to be crucified. Which was the penalty for robbery—and kindred crimes. According to the law of honest people, which does not always take into consideration the fact that a man is starving.

And the Youngest Thief, looking into the judge's stern, down-bent face, made no plea for mercy. Perhaps it was because he had found so little mercy in the world. Perhaps it was because death, at that moment, seemed more merciful than life.

They led him off, bound with leather thongs, to a place of confinement. As he went—in a curiously peaceful way, for one who had been marked for execution—the Youngest Thief heard the shouting of a crowd of people outside the prison walls. The shouting was hoarse, embittered, angry. He won-

dered if the calls were for him. But one of his guards, seeing the look of puzzlement upon his face, roared with laughter.

"It is not for you, scum," he told the Youngest Thief, "that the mob shouts. You are already forgotten! It is the King, this King of the Jews, for whom they cry."

The Youngest Thief was not listening. "King of the Jews," was a term that meant very little to him. Only once had he followed in the train of royalty, when he had entered a small, light-swept town after the caravan of a prince. The Youngest Thief shut his eyes tightly. Not because he was afraid—because he was tired. After a while, his guards left him alone. And all through the night he sat dozing in his cell—and the others, for there were other prisoners—wondered what manner of man he was to take death so lightly.

For, to all appearances, he did take it lightly. On the morrow—even after they had nailed him to a cross, on a hilltop, beyond the city—he did not moan. As a boy he had been trained to bear pain stoically. He had heard of crucifixion—and its agony—as a tiny lad in the desert. The idea was not new. And now, though men had beaten him, he was still a stoic. He would not cry—at least, aloud—at the final flick of the lash! There was something almost gallant in the very droop of his head.

Three crosses there were upon the hilltop. Three crosses that rose, from the crying of the mob, to stand in stark silhouette against a stormy sky. Each of the crosses bore a burden of pain. On the one farther from the Youngest Thief, hung another robber—a dark-browed fellow who spoke in a low, steady stream of blasphemy. And upon the cross between the two of them was pinioned a Man with a pale, finely sensitive face. A Man who wore upon His white brow a crown that had been fashioned of cruel thorns. The Youngest Thief felt a strange sense of pity and concern as he noticed that blood flowed from the wounds that each thorn had made!

There was a stirring at the foot of the middle cross. There were men and women crying, and there were soldiers who fought among themselves. But a curious lassitude was creeping over the body, and into the brain, of the Youngest Thief. And he did not heed the words that were said—did not heed until suddenly the Man upon the middle cross spoke. And His voice was so gentle, so touched—even then—with the wonder of eternal love that the Youngest Thief tried hard to listen. To listen even though his very senses were swooning, though his limbs were numb with pain.

The words that the Man upon the middle cross spoke? After all, they were simple words—words that even a dying thief might understand.

"Father," said the Man—and there was a note, deep and stirring as an organ tone, in the quality of His wonderful voice. "Father, forgive them, for they know not what they do!"

* * * * *

To the Youngest Thief, listening, the voice of the Man brought sudden realization. Sudden and utter calm. This Man—crucified as he was being crucified—was asking that their common tormentors be forgiven. Was saying that they—this mob—did not understand. Perhaps, after all, that was the answer! People—when they were unkind—did not understand. People—when they hurt other people—did it unknowingly. Surely, the Youngest Thief told himself, had they looked into his heart, the years would not have been so

bitter. Surely, had they looked into his striving soul, the world would have trusted and helped. Would have accepted gladly the gift that he had tried to give to a tiny Baby. *The gift of a clean life.*

The other robber, upon the far cross, was speaking, in a tone drenched with hatred. "If Thou be Christ—" he was saying, "save Thyself, and us."

The name "Christ." It was unknown to the Youngest Thief. So, he thought, *was the Man addressed.* But suddenly he found himself speaking. Speaking phrases of rebuke to the robber who taunted. Speaking in a voice of surprising strength. And as he spoke, he turned his head, with a final effort, to gaze upon the Man beside him. And it was then that he saw words printed in three languages upon the middle cross, above the Man's head. And the words read, "This is the King of the Jews."

A King? All at once the Youngest Thief was hearing what the jailer, a day before, had said to explain the noise of an unruly throng beyond the prison walls. And—more. He was seeing a path silvered by a strange, glorious light—a light that had beckoned a youth along a desert way.

It was the memory of that path—leading always toward a King—that gave the Youngest Thief his final courage. He spoke once more—and slowly.

"Lord," he said, and he spoke very softly, very haltingly, "Lord—" oh, each word came with an effort!—"remember me when Thou . . . comest . . . into . . . Thy . . . kingdom."

The Man, there on the middle cross, turned His head until His eyes were level with the eyes of the Youngest Thief. And as their glances crossed, the Youngest Thief knew that at the last—at the very end of the way—he had met with friendship and faith. That his great sacrifice had been worth the price of shame and sorrow. As the Man spoke, the Youngest Thief found that he was scarcely listening to a message of blessed assurance. All at once he was young again, and strong, and free. A boy, standing in the starlight, thinking radiant thoughts.

Somehow, as his eyes closed, the Youngest Thief was seeing a stable place. And a Baby, resting against a mother's breast. And—oh, all at once his soul was thrilling! For something in the Man's warm, enfolding gaze was like a star.

Someone, glancing up from the crowd below, saw—with amazement and unbelief—that a smile lay upon the still lips of the Youngest Thief.

———————————

Margaret E. Sangster Jr. (1894–1981) was an editor, script writer, journalist, short-story writer, and novelist. She was one of the most beloved inspirational writers of the twentieth century.

Plum Pudding for Prosperity

Mabel McKee

Julia Anne was ashamed to admit she'd been a failure in New York. But it was small comfort that the nationwide depression was getting worse every day. Had she been even modestly successful, she could hold her head up high this Christmas.

So what should she do?

* * * * *

To tell John that she was broke would not be an easy task, Julia Anne realized as she hung holly wreaths at all the windows and fastened mistletoe to the chandeliers just as Mother had done through all the years at Christmas time.

Savory, spicy odors filled the whole house. Old Cynthia's recipe books were responsible for these. By following all the directions carefully, Julia Anne had managed to make as tasty mincemeat and as firm and inviting a plum pudding as Cynthia ever had made when she had been cook at the Moulter home.

Cynthia, who had retired from work since her two sons had obtained jobs, had left her clean little cabin for two days, early in the week, to help Julia Anne open the old Moulter home. Her older brother, Doctor John Moulter, had thought it was being opened just for the holidays. His eyes had gleamed joyously when Julia Anne had told him of the plan of having Christmas this year at home instead of at the Lindendale hotel as they had done each year since Mother's death.

Julia Anne wished now that she had said, "I've come home to stay. I'm a failure as an artist. I haven't been able to sell a single sketch or get even an order from an editor. All my money is gone; so I'm going to stay at home."

Worse still, she would have to tell Eric Curry, who had protested her going to New York to try to become an illustrator. She had not come from a successful position in the East, as he had done, to say as he began managing the Curry factory, "It's all the bunk saying there's any other place on this globe equal to Lindendale. Lindendale for me the rest of my life."

As for Christmas, Julia Anne was going to pretend to be merry through Christmas although her heart held the tragedy of being told she was a failure. She had promised Mother always to make Christmas merry for her older brother, John, and for Claude, the youngest of the Moulter family, who was only fifteen.

A sharp rap at the door interrupted the girl's dismal thoughts. It might be Claude, who liked Christmas surprises. Hurriedly, Julia Anne pushed the plum pudding inside the biggest pantry cupboard, smoothed her rumpled dusky curls, and went to open the door.

John was on the side veranda, shaking the snow from his great coat. "Pick-up supper, Judy!" he laughed. "A late operation tonight, and I want to get back as quickly as possible. Claude will soon be here."

A pick-up supper! That meant supper on the kitchen table. Julia Anne hurriedly spread the table, cooked the bacon and eggs, made the toast. John's operation meant relief from his questions about her work, her fellow artists, and so on.

Claude, who arrived in a rush, washed his hands at the kitchen sink. His whistle of surprise over the pick-up supper was followed by a lusty question called out to his brother. "Doc, if I can coax Cynthia back, can't we keep the house open after Christmas? You know you despise that hotel food."

Julia Anne caught the hurried frown with which John hushed Claude. Her insistence, however, made him give the reason why the two brothers could not stay on at the big house. "Finances, Sis," he said soberly. "Didn't mean to tell you until after Christmas. Most of my patients can't pay their bills. The Curry mill is working only one or two days a week. Eric says that if they don't get some big orders soon, they'll have to close down altogether."

Julia Anne's gasp rather appalled John. "Oh, Judy, it isn't that bad," he hurried to add. "There are other industries in Lindendale. I'll just have to enlarge my field. I've always followed Father's example and rather stuck to Elm Street and this neighborhood. Now the Curry Enameling Company is employing most of these people."

Claude boyishly burst in on the conversation then. Eric should have stayed on in the East where he had real opportunities, he declared. If he had done that, he would not be growing thin worrying as he is now doing at home.

"Eric isn't worrying for himself." John's voice was sharp. "He's thinking of that factory his father built, and Lindendale. That factory has meant life to all west Lindendale. Of course it crushes Eric now to see the men and women who

have been employed thirty or more years in the enameling works come to need."

He talked on about the new utilities Eric was trying out at the mill. Too many other companies were manufacturing colored enamelware to make it profitable. If the new roofing was successful, however, the mill would remain at work.

As John slipped into his coat, he turned his conversation toward Christmas Day. "How about a little company, Sis?" he smiled eagerly. "I know it's a shame to let you do all the cooking for us; but since we're to have a Christmas dinner at home, I thought we might have Eric. He's lonely in that big —"

"And how about having Jimmie York?" Claude interrupted, his voice wistful. "He hasn't even a big house."

"The turkey Mr. Dougherty sent us weighs fourteen pounds," laughed Julia Anne. "Two guests are not enough. Why not each of you invite two or three? There's a peach of a plum pudding too."

John whistled his way out of the room, and Julia Anne and Claude were left alone, he to confide boyishly that John liked Christmas parties like the ones they had when Mother was in the big house. Tears came to his eyes as he talked. Boyishly he tried to hide them by offering to wipe the dishes so he would have an excuse to stay in the kitchen where he could smell the pudding.

The closeness to his sister made him confide that John had said he wished Julia Anne could stay in Lindendale, if only she could paint here. "We wouldn't want anything to interfere with your career, Judy," he smiled. "John's terribly proud of your painting. He has that little picture you made of Mother years ago hanging in his office. And sometimes he says that when he is rich, he's going to hire you to paint him a hundred pictures."

"What kind of pictures?" Julia Anne's voice was low.

"Pictures of people and places he loves," explained Claude. "Dad and Mother, the old cabin at the lake, Dad's old car. The doc's funny that way about people and places he loves."

The next morning, Julia Anne took from the great box, which had carried them from New York, her "disappointments," as she termed them; the pictures that had brought her only failure. The most famous art dealer who had seen them had been most kind to her. "No one is buying pictures now," he had said. "Even the best-known artists are having hard sledding."

One picture of which Julia Anne was especially fond, was *Autumn*, a creek scene; the creek in which she and John and Eric had fished. The old art dealer had said the colors in it were almost perfect. Another which had almost made the grade with a magazine editor was a portrait of Mother with Claude's big shepherd dog. Also there was a tiny painting of Father at the wheel of his old car, his medicine case on the seat beside him. Julia Anne had called it, *The Real Physician*.

Other pictures came from the big box—the Christmas dinner one and the painting of Grandmother pouring tea. Julia Anne studied them all for minutes, for hours. Her decision to give these as Christmas gifts had come right after Claude had told how much John thought of her pictures.

She would give some of these pictures to the family friends—old Doctor White, who had once been Father's partner; Cynthia, Mother's cook; and Mrs. Minteer, who had been bedridden so many years. All these people of Lindendale, like John and Claude, thought Julia Anne a real artist.

The portrait of Mother would go to Claude, the one of Father to John for his office. Eric should have the one of Grandmother pouring tea, for close to the teapot was the quaint cookie jar and sandwich plate, which he had termed his "best pals" long ago. Eric, whose own grandparents had died when he was quite tiny, had loved Grandmother very much.

Carefully, she wrapped the pictures in tissue paper, tied them with a gold cord, and tucked in a sprig of holly. That evening she told John that she had decided to give pictures to all the family friends.

"Great, Judy!" he beamed approval. "As I said last night, I'm sort of short of funds now. But I had saved for Christmas. Now we'll take that money and buy shawls for the old women at the county farm, like Dad always did. And we can get caps or something like that for the old men. If there's enough, buy something for the orphanage children."

Julia Anne's dusky eyes gleamed beautifully, happily, contentedly.

* * * * *

Christmas morning had arrived with John and Claude singing out, "Merry Christmas." The gifts were opened next. There was a gay red pocketbook for Julia Anne from Claude and a fur piece from John. "The pelts came from the Warren fox farm," he confided. "They paid for the operation on Mr. Warren and then the fur shop here made them up. Why Judy, darling, how great!"

He had opened his Christmas package. For a long time, he just stood still looking at his father leaning forward over the wheel of his old car, his hand upraised as though to wave at someone, the worn medicine bag beside him.

Before John could say more, Claude was holding the portrait of Mother before him. The youth did not say a word, just hung the portrait above the piano and sat down to look at it, adoration on his face.

"Sometimes you can't say anything, Judy." John found his voice first. "You're too moved."

Breakfast followed, and then the three Moulter children went together to deliver the gifts to old Doctor White, Eric, old Cynthia, and all the others. They shook hands all around with the old people at the county home, and then drove on with their gifts to the orphanage.

They took Julia Anne home after that. While Claude and John were away on the older brother's necessary calls, she flew about getting the dinner ready.

She had just started laying the table when an imperative ring took her to the door. A few minutes later, she was talking with Eric, a taller, thinner Eric than she had known in the old days, and a stranger.

The stranger told her why he had come. He was the head of a chain of stores. The enameling company had been trying to secure a contract from him. He had stopped that morning on his way to a lodge miles farther on to tell Eric he did not like the articles submitted. They were not individual enough to attract customers. He had been there when Eric's Christmas gift, the portrait of Grandmother pouring tea, had arrived.

"I want him to make us some teapots and cookie jars just like those in the picture," he said. "Same pattern, same colors. You're the artist who made them and I've come to see if you'll design some other clever ones for him, quaint jars and bowls that everybody will buy."

He walked about the rooms in the Moulter home, looking at the pictures while Eric talked to Julia Anne. Would she, who painted portraits and landscapes so beautifully, stop this work for a little while to design for the Curry mills? "It will mean work at the mills every day," his eyes shone. "It will—"

Julia Anne turned from him to call the head of the chain stores. "The Curry Enameling Company has just signed me up as designer. Did you say the contract is to be for a year?"

"For five of them if you can keep up this work," he returned. "And let me tell you, young lady, you're wise in turning to designing. I know scores of excellent artists in New York who are starving because they won't take up other work."

* * * * *

The Christmas dinner was just a memory. Eric and the three Moulters were alone, sitting close to the grate, in which the fire had burned low. Eric had stayed after the other guests had left so they could plan for the future.

"The mill's working every day," John suddenly exclaimed. "Why, that will mean we can have all the improvements Dad had planned for the hospital. Isn't it great? And Judy at home—"

Claude jumped up from his chair impulsively. "What say?" he exclaimed. "Let's all go out and sing Christmas carols to Lindendale."

Julia Anne smiled and slipped into her coat. Why, she was not a failure after all, thanks to John, who had wanted her pictures hung everywhere, and to Eric and Claude who had given her courage. As for Lindendale—well, it was the most wonderful town in the world because it was home. It took Christmas to make one realize that!

Mabel McKee was one of America's most popular writers of inspirational stories during the first half of the twentieth century.

A Christmas Gift in Prison

Author Unknown

The governor of the prison, hardened by years of daily contact with evil, turned a deaf ear to the importuning little girl. But then, desperate in her great need, she tried again one last time.

* * * * *

Some years ago, while conducting meetings in Michigan City, I was asked to preach to the convicts in the state prison. I sat on the platform with the governor and watched the prisoners march in—seven hundred men, young and old. They marched in lockstep, every man's hand on the shoulder of the man before him. Among that number were seventy-six "lifers."

After the singing, I arose to preach, but could hardly speak for weeping. Disregarding all the rules of the prison in my earnestness to help the poor fallen men, I left the platform and walked down the aisle among them, taking one and then another by the hand and praying for them. At the end of the row of men who had been committed for murder, sat a man who, more than his fellows, seemed marked by sin's blighting curse. His face was seamed with rigid scars and marks of vice and sin. He looked as though he might be a demon incarnate if aroused to anger. I placed my hand upon his shoulder and prayed for him.

When the service was over, the governor said to me, "Well, Kain, do you know you have broken the rules of the prison by leaving the platform?"

"Yes, governor, but I did want to get close to the poor, despairing fellows, pray for them, and tell them of the love of Jesus who came to seek and to save that which is lost."

"Do you remember," said the governor, "the man at the end of the line in the lifers' row, with whom you prayed? Would you like to hear his history?"

"Yes," I answered gladly.

"Tom Galson was sent here about eight year ago for murder. He was, without doubt, one of the most desperate and vicious characters we ever had and gave us a great deal of trouble.

"One Christmas Eve, about six years ago, I had to spend the night at the prison. Early in the morning, I left the prison, my pockets full of presents for my little girl. It was bitterly cold and I buttoned up my overcoat to protect myself from the cutting wind. As I hurried along, I saw a little girl, wretchedly clothed in a thin dress, her bare feet thrust into a pair of shoes much the worse for wear. In her hand, she held a small parcel. Wondering who she was and why she was out so early in the morning, yet too weary to be interested, I hurried on. Hearing something, I turned and there stood the same wretched-looking girl.

" 'What do you want?' I asked, sharply.

" 'Are you the governor of the prison, sir?'

" 'Yes, who are you, and why are you not at home?'

" 'Please, sir; I have no home; Mama died in the poorhouse two weeks ago, and just before she died, she said Papa was in prison, and she thought maybe he would like to see his little girl. Please, can't you let me see my papa? Today is Christmas, and I want to give him a present.'

" 'No,' I replied gruffly, 'you will have to wait until visitors' day.'

"I had not gone many steps when I felt a pull at my coat, and a pleading voice said, 'Please, don't go.'

"I stopped and looked into the pinched, beseeching face. Great tears were in her eyes, while her chin quivered with emotion.

" 'Mister,' she said, 'if your little girl was me, and your girl's mama had died in the poorhouse and her papa was in prison, and she had no place to go and no one to love her, don't you think she would like to see her papa? If it was Christmas and your little girl came to see me, if I was governor of the prison and asked me to please let her see Papa and give him a Christmas present, don't you—don't you think I would say yes?'

"By this time, a great lump was in my throat and my eyes were swimming in tears. I answered, 'Yes, my little girl, I think you would, and you shall see your papa.'

"Taking her hand, I hurried back to the prison, thinking of my own fair-haired little girl at home. Arriving in my office, I asked her to come near the warm stove, while I sent a guard to bring number thirty-seven from his cell. As soon as he came into the office and saw the little girl, his face clouded with an angry frown, and in a gruff, savage tone, he snapped out, 'Nellie, what are you doing here? What do you want? Go back to your mother.'

" 'Please, Papa,' sobbed the little girl, 'Mama's dead. She died two weeks ago in the poorhouse, and before she died she told me to take care of little Jimmie, 'cause you loved him so. She told me to tell you she loved you too—but Papa—' and her voice broke in sobs and tears, 'Jimmie died, too, last week, and now I am alone, Papa, and today's Christmas, Papa, and I thought maybe as you loved Jimmie, you would like a little Christmas present from him.'

"Here she unrolled the little package she held in her hand until she came to a little package of tissue paper, from which she took a little hair curl, and put it in her father's hand, saying, 'I cut it from dear little Jimmie's head, Papa, just before they buried him.'

"Number thirty-seven by this time was sobbing like a child, and so was I. Stooping down, he picked up the little girl, pressed her convulsively to his breast, while his great frame shook with suppressed emotion.

"The scene was too sacred for me to look upon, so I softly opened the door and left them alone. In about an hour, I returned. Number thirty-seven sat near the stove with his little daughter on his knee. He looked at me sheepishly for a moment and then said, 'Governor, I haven't any money.' Then suddenly stripping off his prison jacket, he said, 'Don't let my little girl go out this bitter cold day with that thin dress. Let me give her this coat. I'll work early and late; I'll do anything. I'll be a man. Please, governor, let me cover her with this coat.' Tears were streaming down the face of the hardened man.

" 'No, Galson,' I said, 'keep your coat; your little girl shall not suffer. I'll take her to my home and see what my wife can do for her.'

" 'God bless you,' sobbed Galson.

"I took the girl into my home. She remained with us a number of years and became a true Christian by faith in the Lord Jesus Christ. Tom Galson also became a new creature in Christ and then he gave us no more trouble."

* * * * *

When I visited the prison again, the governor said to me, "Kain, would you like to see Tom Galson, whose story I told you a few years ago?"

"Yes, I would." The governor took me down a quiet street, stopped at a neat home, and knocked at the door. The door was opened by a cheerful young woman who greeted the governor with the utmost cordiality.

We went in and the governor introduced me to Nellie and her father who, because of his reformation, had received a pardon. He was now living an upright Christian life with his daughter, whose little Christmas gift had broken his hard heart.

The Christmas Substitute

Anna Sprague Packard

A boy of the streets was Teddy Fitzgerald. And now, at Christmas, he was in the house of God for the very first time. And the music—such music as he'd never heard!

And then . . . the great temptation.

* * * * *

The choir room of St. Martin's Cathedral was nearly full of boys arrayed in black cassocks and white cottas. The processional cross with its bunch of holly tied to it, leaned against the wall. From the church could be heard the strains of *Messiah*, and through the open door of the vestry room the choirmaster could see the clergy all ready to move.

"Why, where's Charley Reed?" asked one of the singers.

"I sent him off for a substitute to fill Johnny Healey's place," answered the choirmaster. "Charley said he knew a boy who had a good voice, so I let him go. I wish I hadn't."

"Is he first in the 'Te Deum'?"

"Yes, and—oh, here he is!"

Charley Reed stood in the doorway ushering in the substitute—a boy perhaps ten or twelve years of age, distinctly dirty. He wore an old jacket and a pair of trousers much too large. His shoes were breaking apart, and he held in his hand an old cap, which had once been fur, but was now only skin. It was not his poverty alone that marked him, however. It was his face—cool, cunning, impudent, a face that before twenty must acquire the criminal look of life. A cadet in the ranks of the dangerous class, he stood there, self-possessed, confidently, slyly alert.

The choirmaster hurried forward with an evident attempt to make the best of the situation. In a few moments, robed in his vestment and with a clean face and hands, Teddy Fitzgerald, the East Side boy, stood in his place in the line, an open hymnal in his hand.

The boy with the cross took his place at the head of the procession. The clergy came down the steps into the choir room. There was a short program, a quick "amen" chanted by the boys, and then the first verse of "Adeste Fideles." As the music soared joyfully and triumphant, the procession began to move.

The doors of the choir room were thrown back, the great organ took up the theme, and Teddy Fitzgerald was in the house of God—for the first time.

Churches had been quite outside Teddy's life. In the summertime, he had stolen his way to several Sunday School picnics. Once, with an older gang of roughs, he had gone to help break up the Salvation Army meeting; but these had been his sole encounters with religion.

And now here he was—a heathen in a long black cassock and snow-white cotta, his face radiant with joy, keeping perfect time as the long line swept through the transept and into the chancel.

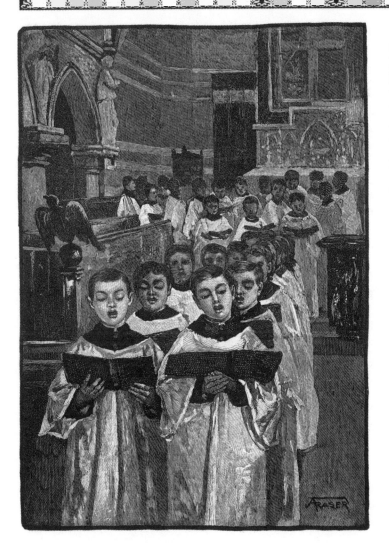

The boys filed decorously into the stalls. Teddy's seat was on the end with Charley Reed beside him. During the service, Charley would nudge him to kneel, sit, or stand as the occasion demanded, and Teddy obeyed implicitly. When the chanting of the Psalms began, Teddy took his first active part. They were Gregorian chants full of a solemn joy, and the boy quickly caught the movement, for he loved music passionately.

He had never heard any really great music before. The best had been at the Central Park concerts on Saturday afternoons, when the child would sit, wrapped in that bliss which only a musical soul can know.

One masterpiece followed another today; the "Te Deum" and then the "Creed." Charley Reed had solos in both. Teddy listened greedily, enviously.

I bet yer I could do it if I only knew how! I bet yer I could put more "go" into her! With critical instinct he had found the lack in Charley Reed's beautiful voice— the inability to touch the heart.

Then followed some prayers, and then a carol. They were printed on the service list and Teddy read, "O Little Town of Bethlehem." He wondered vaguely where the town was, and what there could be to write about it. If it had been a big city, that would have been another thing—but just a little town!

He listened through the first verse; then with the second, he began to sing. The choirmaster heard the clear, full tones, and listened with fear. Would he sing a false note and ruin it? No, Teddy was as incapable of singing false as a bird is. Above the choir, above even Charley Reed's sweet soprano, rang the contralto with its rare, pathetic quality—that something which can never be acquired—and the congregation listened with their hearts.

During the sermon, Teddy looked around at the wonderful pictured window through which the Christmas sun was streaming, the fine lines of arch and roof, the carved stalls, the shining marble altar with its gleaming cross, and above it a picture which caught and held his eye—the picture of a Child—a boy with outstretched arms, coming toward him through a field of lilies.

All through the service there had been a name repeated which was horribly familiar to the boy and he had wondered as he had seen the bowed heads. This must be He then! Someone to be worshiped; Someone who had suffered. So he gazed at the picture with longing in his keen eyes.

Why, He is a boy and coming toward me. I wish He wouldn't look at me like that! Seems as if He wanted me to do something for Him. Kinder sorry too. Looks like He'd lived on the East Side, so poor and mournful. I bet you He knows what it is to be cold and hungry, and sleep in a barrel! I wish now I hadn't knocked down that little kid this mornin' or cheated Jim at craps. And so, while the good doctor preached in the pulpit, the boy above the altar preached to the boy below.

Suddenly Charley Reed said, "I say Teddy, you'll have to go and receive the contribution. I sing a solo in the offertory. Follow the boy at the end of the opposite stall, keep step with him, march to the rail, and the doctor will give you both plates. Then turn—be sure you wheel toward the other boy—march to the top of the steps and wait. Stand perfectly still, and the vestrymen will bring up the offering. Then wheel inside, carry the plates and empty them into the alms basin the doctor will hold. Do just as Tom does, keep step, and oh! don't bungle, for then they will blame me!"

Charley did not know his boy. Teddy bungle! He marched in perfect time, shoulder to shoulder, and stood facing the vast congregation.

Two by two the vestrymen came up, each emptying his full plate into the larger ones held by the boys. Would they never stop? What heaps of money! Teddy had never seen so much—and now he was holding it!

Such a chance! Right behind his thumb lay a bill folded very small. Some lady must have tucked it in her glove. Just as he wheeled, he put his thumb on it and with a dextrous movement, he concealed it in his palm. Teddy had not played craps for nothing.

He went back to his stall, flushed with a sense of triumph, and tucked the bill into his jacket pocket. He must not look at it yet. It might be a fiver! Wouldn't he blow her in!

All the while the service was going on, but it was only the opening notes of Gounod's "Sanctus" that brought him back.

As the first "Holy, Holy" stole out, he forgot his money and all the glories that it could buy. Again and again rang out the marvelous cry, each repetition stronger and nearer the throne, and the heart of the boy went with it.

He looked at the picture with a radiant smile. This must surely make Him glad! The sunshine fell on the calm face; it lighted up those eyes filled with inscrutable sorrow and a pang struck into Teddy's heart like a knife. *The money!* He had taken it from Him! And as he laid his head down on the stall, beside which he knelt, an agony rocked him, which no hunger or cold or pain had forced from him. Teddy Fitzgerald's soul was being born.

The service ended and the procession moved out of the church and into the choir room once more. "Here's fifty cents," said the choirmaster. "Come around tomorrow at nine and let me try your voice. I think you have a fortune there!" But the words seemed to fall on deaf ears. Teddy turned away and went out into the street, still holding the service sheet in his hand.

That same evening, as the rector of St. Martin's rose from the Christmas dinner, a servant entered the room to say a policeman was in the hall waiting to see him.

"Sorry to disturb you, sir, but there's a boy been asking for you at the Bellevue Hospital, and as the doctors say he won't live till morning, that's why, I've come for you. He's just been run over by a car on Third Avenue."

Before long, the doctor was leaning over the poor, crushed frame of Teddy Fitzgerald lying in the first fine, white bed he had ever known.

"Gimme de money," said the boy to the nurse beside him, "and then go away!" The nurse obeyed and the doctor knelt beside the bed to hear the words:

"Here it is! Give it back to Him! I swiped it this morning out of your collection plate. All the afternoon I tried to spend it and I couldn't. I could see Him a-lookin' at me—Him behind the altar, a-comin' through the lily field after me! So I was comin' back with it to you, when I was hurt. Please believe me—'tain't because I know it's all up with me that I'm sorry, but—because I couldn't be such a sneak to Him. You see, He was like me. He had lots against Him!"

The doctor's white head sank, and he prayed, holding the grimy, bony hand which had fought the world from the start.

The little life was drifting fast now and he was babbling of many things; but never of home or mother! The streets! Their length, their heat, their chill, but always the streets. It was all his past. Suddenly, his faltering voice began to sing,

"O little town of Bethlehem, how still we see thee
    lie!
Above thy deep and dreamless sleep the silent stars
    go by.
Yet in thy dark street shineth the everlasting Light;
The hopes and fears of all the years are met in thee
    tonight."

A rapturous look came into the dying eyes, and Teddy Fitzgerald passed out of this world of sorrow.

———————————

Anna Sprague Packard wrote for popular and inspirational magazines during the first half of the twentieth century.

And Glory Shone All Around

Christine Whiting Parmenter

All too often, Christmas celebrations in our homes and towns turn out to be selfish—and self-centered. Nobody, it seems, is much interested in making sure the unpopular, the disadvantaged, the crippled, the caregivers who give up their own Christmas plans in order to care for those incapable of giving back, are remembered.

Back when this was written (almost a century ago), those burdened by an all-too-common affliction we today label "Alzheimer's" or "dementia" were then referred to as "silly," "foolish," or "childish."

This wondrous story by the author of "David's Star of Bethlehem," once read is mighty hard to forget.

* * * * *

It wasn't until two years ago that our town indulged in a community Christmas tree, and though it may be wicked to remember such a thing now that all's serene again, that tree was responsible for a perfectly fearful row. It was Dr. Gardner who started it—not the row, of course, but the Christmas tree. He asked all the ministers in town, and one or two others, including Father Gallagher, the priest at St. Francis's, to meet at his house one evening in December, and then he suggested that we have a real, live tree on Christmas eve, with all the church choirs in town to lead the carols.

Of course, this idea wasn't original with Dr. Gardner, but it was new to us, and those men just ate it up. I suppose they were fired with the Christmas spirit, for when Mr. Stanley, the Baptist minister and an old dear, suggested using the wonderful blue spruce on his church green, they all agreed it was the very thing, the Baptist church being in a central location, and the tree, which was imported from Colorado years ago, being the handsomest specimen in town.

But they had counted without some of their parishioners, who, if they ever had any Christmas spirit, promptly forgot it in jealousy of their brother Baptists. For days it looked as if there wouldn't be any community tree at all! Dr. Gardner told Dad that he was mentally black and blue from contact with the numerous people who stopped him on every corner to present their views on the subject. Of course, he had plenty of sympathizers, but a small element in a town like ours can make a lot more noise than the bigger element that behaves itself; and things crackled.

It was Father Gallagher who poured oil on the troubled waters by suggesting that we use one of the big cedars on the common. This cleared the air, and people who had been hardly speaking to each other for a week became neighborly once more, and the Christmas spirit was again rampant.

Despite all the trouble it had caused, that tree was a huge success. As Bill Raney said, the whole thing looked like an old-fashioned Christmas card. There'd been a light snow that morning, and everything was glistening in the starlight. The tree was a glory (thanks to Mr. Edison's electric lights!), and every one of the houses facing the common had rows of lighted candles in its windows. It seemed, too, as if everybody in town must be there. It wasn't till afterward that I realized—

You see, it was this way. I'd lost Dad and Mother in the crowd and was wondering where they were when Bill Raney tapped me on the shoulder.

"Come on, Kit. The old folks are over at the Gardners', and I promised to hunt you up. I'll take you home after I leave one of Mother's baskets for Lizzie Collins. It's late, but she never locks her door, so if things are dark, I'll slip it right inside. My flivver's parked back of the Town Hall. All modern improvements to the contrary, I almost wish it was a horse and sleigh, a night like this! Isn't the whole thing corking?"

It was. We stopped right there and looked back at that gorgeous tree with the star-flecked sky above it. The throng was dispersing, but a crowd of Girl Scouts had got together and, as they walked along, were singing, "God Rest Ye Merry, Gentlemen." It was then that Bill said it looked like an old-fashioned Christmas card; and it did. Though I had a million last things to do at home, I turned away almost reluctantly.

Well, we hopped into the flivver and started toward East Avenue, which is the nearest thing to slums that our town possesses. I was holding the basket for Lizzie Collins on my lap, and said, "Wasn't Liz at the Christmas tree, Bill?"

Lizzie is one of our town's priceless assets—a woman who'll do anything on earth from minding a baby to getting a good dinner at a moment's notice. We couldn't exist without Liz.

"Nope," said Bill. "She's afraid to leave her father alone evenings now he's so childish; and didn't want to ask anyone to stay with him the night of the tree. Mother found it out this afternoon and offered to look after the old man herself, but Lizzie wouldn't let her."

"Well," said I, "it was pretty nice of your mother to offer. I'd hate like anything to nurse-maid old man Collins—especially on Christmas Eve."

Bill chuckled. "You ought to have heard Dad on the subject! He said to Mother, 'Do you imagine for one moment that I'd have allowed you to stay alone in that locality guarding a crazy man?' Of course, old man Collins isn't what you'd call crazy; but Dad was wild. I owe Liz a vote of thanks for refusing that offer, for I'd have been obliged to accompany Mother as a bodyguard. Dad had a date with the Unitarian choir, you know."

Bill's father has a wonderful tenor voice and is always roped in when there's any singing to be done.

"Just the same," I repeated, "it was sweet of your mother to even think of such a plan. Here we are, and the house is lighted too. I guess I'll go in with you and wish Lizzie a Merry Christmas."

East Avenue runs along by the railroad tracks. It's usually black and sooty, but the snow had covered the soot that night and Liz had some wreaths in the windows, so it looked quite Christmasy, all except a freight train that was shunting back and forth on the tracks behind her cottage. Bill rapped, and Lizzie came to the door.

"Glory be!" she exclaimed; "Are you half froze? Come in and warm up. Father's in bed, and I was just fillin' the stockin's."

We went into her tiny, neat sitting room, and Bill laid the basket on the table. It was a beautiful basket with a smashing red bow on the handle. I could just imagine the lovely things

Mrs. Raney had packed inside. Bill explained that his mother sent it, and Lizzie went into a eulogy on Mrs. Raney's virtues, while I glanced curiously about the room.

I hadn't seen that room for years, and for a moment I couldn't understand why it looked familiar. Then I suddenly realized that it was almost entirely furnished with things that the people Liz worked for had given her. There was the Toppings's old music stand—some kind of black wood with gilt decorations and little gilt chains hanging in festoons from the top shelf. There was a red glass vase that used to be in Dot Meadows's living room (I simply adored it when I was a kid), and the patent rocker that old Mrs. Reese insisted on using till the day of her death, though it was a perfect eyesore and the whole family implored her to give it up. On the mantel were two cut-glass cologne bottles, with bows of orange satin ribbon tied around their necks, that had once occupied the place of honor in the Sawyers's guest room. I'd wager the ribbons hadn't been changed in twenty years! And over the sofa (a worn leather affair that was in Dr. Gardner's office when I was in kindergarten), there hung a steel engraving of some children playing seesaw, exactly like one that hung in my grandmother's house at Portland. I saw the same thing in Willie's room when I went to the movie *Abraham Lincoln,* and I stayed through two shows just to see it again. I always *loved* that picture at Grand-

ma's. I was just going to ask Liz where she got it, when my eye lit on the stockings she was filling: a black cotton one and a man's cheap gray sock; but Bill, who evidently spied them at the same moment, asked in surprise:

"Why, Liz, have you got company for Christmas?"

"Yes," answered Lizzie, smiling, "I got myself, which is sometimes poor company, dear knows; and I got the child that the good Lord gave me in my old age."

She lifted the sock and we both knew she meant that her poor old father was just a child again. I guess neither of us knew what to say, but Liz didn't give us a chance to say anything. She began to show us the things she'd got for her father's stocking—just little ten-cent-store toys and picture books and a cheap handkerchief with blue border.

"Yes, he's a child now," she said sadly. "I wish I could have taken him to the tree tonight. He'd have enjoyed it, Father would. He was a grand singer in his day too. He'd have loved the carols; but his legs is old if his head ain't, and he couldn't have walked so far in the slippery goin'. Well, you thank yer mother for the basket, Bill," Liz has worked for our mothers since before we were born, and calls us all by our first names, "and wish her a Merry Christmas; and you, too, Katherine."

We were pretty quiet as we started back. I couldn't seem to get Lizzie Collins out of my mind—alone there in her little rummage sale of a room, filling her own stocking, and buying ten-cent-store toys for that old man. When we reached the common again, the tree was still lighted, and Bill stopped the car and leaned over on the steering wheel, staring at it.

"Look here!" he said suddenly. "Why didn't somebody bring Lizzie and old man Collins down here in an auto?"

"For the usual reason," I answered. "Nobody *thought*."

"I suppose there are others too," said Bill, after a moment.

"Plenty," said I. "I've been thinking of 'em for ten minutes."

"It would have been more to the point," remarked Bill bluntly, as he took his foot slowly off the brake, "if you'd thought of 'em twenty-four hours ago."

If this sounded rude, I didn't care, because I knew that Bill was really blaming himself every bit as much as he blamed me. And just then Dr. Gardner came out, spied the flivver, and called us in. Sue Gardner was home from college for the holidays, and some of the crowd had drifted over there after the tree. It's always jolly at the Gardners', so for once we obeyed the doctor's orders with light hearts. We piled out joyously, and for the time being forgot all about Lizzie Collins and her poor old father who was "just a child."

* * * * *

Everyone talked about that tree for weeks afterward. They seemed to forget the row it had caused to start with, and said what a wonderful thing it was to see all the townspeople together on Christmas Eve, how splendidly the choirs had led the carols, and "Wasn't it just like Dr. Gardner to suggest it?" You'd have thought to hear them go on that every inhabitant of the town had been present; but I couldn't help thinking of those who couldn't be there: Lizzie Collins and her old father, who'd have enjoyed it as much as anyone; Tommy Hollis, fifteen, and almost helpless from infantile paralysis; some of the old folks at the home, and—oh, a dozen others who'd have given almost anything to have been a part of that Christmas gathering. I vowed that next year I'd do something about it;

but after a while, it slipped out of my mind the way things will, and another Christmas was almost due before I gave it a thought.

Even then it was Bill Raney who brought up the subject. He appeared one evening when Dot Meadows's father and mother were playing bridge with my parents. Dot had come with them, and Sue Gardner had just dropped in with Bob Sawyer. Sue's older than the rest of us, but she's never been one bit snippy the way some older girls are. She'd graduated from Vassar in June and announced her engagement to Bob, at which the whole town rejoiced, because, besides leaving an arm in France, Bob has had a terribly unhappy life, and it seemed too good to be true that he'd won the loveliest girl our town possesses.

We were sitting around the fire when Bill walked in without even knocking.

"Hello, everybody," he said cheerfully. "I'm forced to escape a committee meeting that occupies all my pet lounging places at home. Hope I'm not butting in on anything private?"

"As if you'd care if you were!" retorted Dot; and I said, "I needn't tell you to make yourself at home, Bill. You'll do it anyway. What cruel committee meeting has driven you out into the cold world?"

Bill had turned away to shake hands with the "old folks." Whatever his shortcomings, I'll have to admit that he never forgets his manners; that is, his manners to our fathers and mothers. Mrs. Meadows declares that Bill is the one bright spot in the younger generation; and even Mother, who's unusually up-to-date, says there are moments when she thinks so too.

"What's the committee?" I asked again, as Bill came back and slumped down between Dot and Bob.

"A delegation of choirmasters," he grinned, "planning a program for the community Christmas tree. I left them gravely discussing which of the old reliable carols to start off with. You'd think the fate of nations depended on the correct choice. Are those cookies meant to satisfy the inner man, Kit, or just for ornament?"

"Trust Bill to scent out the edibles!" said Bob, and shoved the plate of cookies nearer. "To think that a whole year has passed since that glorious gathering on the common! Barring infants and invalids, I believe the whole town must have been there."

"It wasn't," said Bill, and his eyes came straight to mine. "Have you forgotten, Kit?"

I shook my head, while, suddenly, it all came back—Lizzie Collins's queer little sitting room and that old gray sock she was filling for her father—I even heard the shunting of the freight train behind the cottage—and realized that only a scant half mile away that gorgeous Christmas tree, which was really Lizzie's tree as much as ours, was lifting its branches to the sky.

"Tell 'em about it, Katherine," said Bill quietly.

I did. I told them of our call on Lizzie last Christmas Eve—of old man Collins's "grand voice," and how he'd have loved to hear the carols. I mentioned Tommy Hollis, and old Mrs. Littlefield, over on the turnpike, and—well—I guess I got "warmed up," as Bill would say. Anyway, when I finished, I was appalled to find that the bridge game had apparently ceased and the four elders were listening to my impassioned speech. It was Bob Sawyer who said regretfully, "How could we ever have forgotten people like that—at Christmastime?"

"There are more Christmases to come," said Bill.

"If Dot will drive one of our cars," broke in Mr. Meadows unexpectedly, "I'll take the other. We can accommodate twelve."

We all turned and stared at the poor man. Mr. Meadows writes fearfully highbrow books and is terribly shy. Sometimes, he acts afraid even of us kids. Now, as he saw all our eyes turned, his way, he blushed furiously; but Dad, who roomed with him at Harvard ages ago, slapped him on the back and said, "Good work, old sport! Now let's get down to business."

This we proceeded to do. Sue agreed to consult her father and get a list of invalids who were able to go out if somebody would only take them. Bill thought of the poor farm, called up the matron, and reported that "fourteen old derelicts were eligible for transportation." For the next week we did nothing except beg or borrow cars and rope in everyone who wasn't already captured by the carol singers' brigade. Young and old seemed bewitched by the idea. Madam Van Arden sent word that her nephew would drive a limousine; and Buster Meadows, Dot's fourteen-year-old brother, was thrilled at the chance to run the Raney's flivver and escort three paupers and old Mrs. Littlefield who weighs two hundred!

That ten days was the most hectic time of my whole life. We lived in mortal terror of forgetting somebody. Sue said afterward that she was haunted by the thought, and lay awake nights while she proceeded mentally down every street in town interviewing the inhabitants.

And then, when our plans were all completed, we began to worry about the weather. Suppose it rained? Suppose a blizzard should rage and the cars wouldn't run? Suppose the electricity went off and the tree wouldn't light? This last cheerful suggestion came from old Mr. Sparrow at the home for the aged, who always looks on the bright side!

None of these things did happen, of course. Bill declare that the night was even better than the year before—better for our purpose, anyway, because it wasn't so cold and the old folks would be more comfortable. It was a gay procession that started out that evening. For the first time in my life, I regretted the fact that in my own hometown I'm considered the possessor of a "remarkable voice." I was roped in by one of the choirs and couldn't drive a car.

Later, however, I didn't mind so much, because I had a wonderful chance to view the whole proceeding. We'd arranged for the cars to park on the north side of the common in front of the high school, and when things got going, Bob Sawyer (who sings baritone in our choir) and I slipped away to wish a Merry Christmas to the occupants of those automobiles.

The Christmas spirit was certainly abroad that night. I couldn't refrain from smiling to see Chauncey Van Arden, a Harvard senior, and so snippy that he won't recognize us high-school girls at all, with his four-thousand-dollar limousine filled with inmates from the poor farm! He even had one of them beside him—a toothless old man who joined in the carol singing with vim and appeared to be having the very time of his life.

Sue Gardner was there with a crowd of ex-service men from her father's sanatorium; and Bill was driving the Toppings's Packard. He had old man Collins beside him, while Lizzie sat behind with Tommy Hollis, Mr. Sparrow, who can't go about except in a wheelchair, blind Colonel Hinkley, our only surviving Civil War veteran, and an old lady from the home.

I tell you, it was something to remember, going down that line. The rector of St. Ann's was driving a furniture truck, and Father Gallagher a milk wagon! Dot Meadows had a car full of crippled children from the Catholic Convalescent Home;

while her father seemed to have forgotten his shyness and was behaving like a regular Beau Brummell to Matilda Bashford, who has a face like a dried lemon, and who, he told us later, hadn't been away from her house on the mountain road for two whole years.

There's no use trying to describe all those people and the joy they showed in being a part of that Christmas party. I had a silly lump in my throat when Bob and I turned back to join the carol leaders beside the tree. Mother and Dad were both acting as chauffeurs, and I expected to walk along home with Mr. Raney; but when everything was over, Bill spied me in the crowd and beckoned.

"Squeeze in somewhere behind, Kit," he suggested. "There's always room for one more on Christmas Eve."

"Sure!" exclaimed Lizzie. "You can sit on my lap, Katherine. You don't weigh nothin'."

"It was a grand sight, wasn't it?" said Mr. Sparrow, leaning forward eagerly. "I ain't had such a time since I was a seven-year-old and my mother made me a birthday cake with candles."

"Wa'n't it a beautiful tree?" piped up Mrs. Loomis. "I never expected to see anythin' so pretty as them lights. I wish you could have seen it, Colonel Hinkley," she added with genuine regret.

"I felt it," answered the colonel, gently. "And this boy," he laid a hand on Tommy Hollis's poor useless knees, "has given me a word picture of it that is very real. And I heard the carols—those beautiful carols that my mother used to sing on Christmas Eve. We never tire of them, do we?"

"You bet we don't!" Tommy's thin face was glowing. "I—I'd rather sing than do most anything!"

"Well," said Lizzy, drawing a deep breath of contentment, "I dunno when I ever *had* such a good time."

Only Bill and the old child beside him remained silent. We reached the home and dropped Mr. Sparrow and Mrs. Loomis, left Colonel Hinkley at his boarding place, and went on a mile to a tiny bungalow where Bill got out and carried Tommy in.

"Merry Christmas, folks!" called Tommy, cheerfully as they went up the path; but all I could think of was the pitiful difference in the bodies of those two boys, and what a sturdy youngster Tommy had been three years before.

"Merry Christmas, old man!" Bill called as he got in once more by Mr. Collins. He waved to Tommy, who was at the window, and then we started again, toward East Avenue this time and Lizzie's little house.

It looked, I thought as we drew nearer, just as it had a year before. It might have been the same freight train shunting noisily on the railroad tracks; and the same bright stars shone overhead. Bill slowed up beside the narrow sidewalk, stopped the car, got out, and with the gallantry he would have bestowed upon a royal princess, helped Lizzie to alight.

"Thanks, Bill," she said gently. "I—I dunno just what to say, but it's been fine, seein' things without standin' on my two feet. And Father—he *sang*, Bill! Did you notice? He sang twice. He had a grand voice when he was young. Maybe he's dropped asleep. Sometimes he does if I don't put him to bed real early. Come, Father, we're home."

I had stepped out on the sidewalk beside Lizzie, and we were all watching the old man. He did indeed seem asleep, but I think he was only dreaming. Anyway, at his daughter's voice, he turned, and Bill helped him down while Lizzie put a steadying arm about him as he stood there on the sidewalk.

"Good night," said Bill, and then paused because the old

man had raised his arm. The childish expression had entirely left his eyes, and something about him made me think of a prophet. He was pointing north, where a sudden burst of sparks from the engine on the freight train had, for the moment, cast a glow over the sky. He said, his deep voice trembling with emotion:

"The angel of the Lord came down, and glory shone around."

I tell you, it sounded awfully strange and solemn. My eyes met Bill's, and I knew he was thinking, just as I was, that this was something we were never going to forget—that white-haired old man with his hand stretched up toward the weirdly lighted heavens, and how those old, old words had come back to him out of a clouded past. I guess none of us could have spoken in that moment, any more than we'd have spoken out loud in church; and just then the silvery notes of the town clock chimed the hour.

It was Christmas morning!

Christine Whiting Parmenter (1877–1953) was born in Plainfield, New Jersey. During the first half of the twentieth century, she was considered to be one of America's leading writers of stories and novels for popular and inspirational magazines. Among her books are titles such as *One Wide River to Cross*, *The Kings of Beacon Hill*, and *Stories of Courage and Devotion*.

The Clock of Life

Joseph Leininger Wheeler

> The clock of life is wound but once,
> And no one can tell you just when the hands will stop
> At late or early hour;
> Now is the only time you have;
> Live, love, toil with a will;
> Place no confidence in tomorrow
> For the clock may then be still.
>
> —Author Unknown

W hale spouting ahead! Starboard at three o'clock." *The Summit* seems to tilt as passengers race to that side of the ship. Among them is a tall man of six feet one inch, with just enough gray in his hair to look distinguished and just enough dark brown to still appear young. By his side, a vivacious blonde is intently watching the breaching whale through her high-powered binoculars.

After the whale disappears in the gathering mist, the couple walks forward to the bow of the ship. They neither hold hands nor walk close to each other—and their words are few. Spoken words, that is.

It's just not working—this cruise. Here I am striding into the wind, reveling in this dream come true in Alaskan waters, but Richard is far away from me. When the church gave us this twenty-fifth anniversary present, I was ecstatic. Finally, something to bring

us together again! Love . . . once we had so much of it, and every day was a new adventure. A lifetime seemed far too short a time to spend with him. Had we been blessed with children, perhaps we'd have remained close. Instead, ever so gradually we drifted apart. Don't really know why or when—I just know that the man silently walking by my side is not the man I once knew. Or thought I knew. Are all marriages like this, I wonder? Gradually growing away from each other. Choosing different paths. Exhibiting character traits not revealed early on—ah, that's the rub! That's what bothers me most. Does he realize how disappointed I am in him? In us? How disillusioned? Of course he must! For I can't help but show it, for always I've worn my heart on my sleeve: my face and eyes give me away every time. Can't hide my thoughts like Richard does.

* * * * *

N ice of the church to give us this cruise—but I'm bored already. Bored by the wildlife, bored by the passengers, bored by the day-trips, even bored—dare I admit it—by Laura. Let's face it, life bores me. I once thought that if I could just get Laura to say Yes, I'd be happy. Or if I could graduate at the top of my class. Or be hired on as a pastor by the district. Or be called to a bigger church—or a bigger yet. All of these dreams have come true, but I'm not happy. I'm bored. Now that I've got the biggest church in the state, I'm still not satisfied. If I get this promised televangelist job—no, I know I'll soon be bored there too. Life itself seems to have lost its savor. Laura just doesn't understand me or my frustrations. She's so, so placid. Happy, always happy—stupidly so, I might add. Or . . . at least she used to be. Come to think of it, I haven't heard her laugh as often as* *she used to. Doesn't smile at me very often anymore. Not even on this cruise. What's happening to her? I wonder sometimes if I married the wrong woman. But in my line of work, divorce is out of the question.*

Queen Charlotte Sound and south

Laura is unable to sleep. Ever so quietly, so as not to awaken Richard, she gets out of bed, dons one of the ship's warm bathrobes, and slips out to the veranda. Oh! the heavenly sound of waves breaking out from the prow of the ship! How luminous the resulting whitecaps reflecting the radiance of a full moon. Settling into a lounge chair and wrapping an alpaca blanket around her, she sets her mind adrift and is lulled to sleep by the music of the sea.

Then . . . her life is changed by one cry:

"Laura!—where *are* you?"

"Out here on the veranda—why?"

"I don't feel well . . . and I'm almost certain I'm running a fever."

"I'll be right in."

Running her hand over his forehead, Laura declares, "My goodness! You *do* have a fever. When did this come on?"

"Oh, sometime during the last hour—I've got the chills too—just can't seem to stop the shaking."

* * * * *

Daylight comes, and a doctor is called in, but he can do little but sedate the patient. All that day, Laura remains by her husband's side.

Night falls, but Richard's condition remains unchanged. The night drags along on turtle feet. It is a little after 2:00 A.M. when Laura ventures out to the veranda in order to gain a little rest.

As the ship makes its way south, and ties up at West Coast ports, Laura sighs because they've scheduled (and pre-paid for) land tours in each area. Each time the ship docks, she asks Richard if he's well enough for her to join that day's tour—and each time he petulantly answers, "No! I might need you!" When Laura reminds him that all he needs to do is buzz the room attendant, and help will be there in only minutes, he bullheadedly refuses to even consider it. So it is that Vancouver Island, Astoria, San Francisco, and Avalon on beautiful Catalina Island are each left behind, with not even one memory to show for it.

By San Francisco, Richard is enough improved to warrant his releasing Laura—but does not. Nor does he in Avalon, though he is now up and walking around, "No, if I don't feel up to taking a tour, you shouldn't go either!"

Finally, Richard and Laura wake up in San Diego harbor. The two-week cruise is over.

The unwelcome visitor

Back home, life resumes its normal pace—with one dif-ference. The flu (what the ship doctor had called it) returns, as regular as clockwork, every month for five to seven days, laying siege to Richard. It never affects Laura. Then, each time, it leaves.

Just when the pattern starts to look ominous, the visitations cease. Thanksgiving comes and goes, as does Christmas. Then

what a relief when January, February, and March come and go without interruption. Meanwhile, Richard continues to preach in his megachurch, and an even greater televangelism opportunity looms on the horizon.

Though Richard is still bored by life, his church, and Laura, that boredom cannot but be tinged by fear: fear that "it" (that flulike something) may return for yet another visit.

It does. Beginning in April, "it" returns with alarming regularity every six weeks, the symptoms the same as before, each time leaving as mysteriously as it came. Though Laura urges him to see a doctor, he avoids doing so. "Perhaps this time 'it' will stay away," he often counters (but less hopefully each time).

It does not. By early September it has come to stay, only this time accompanied by the most terrible unrelenting bodywide itch Richard has ever experienced—and no lotion known to man can do a thing about it! His skin begins to discolor. Now thoroughly alarmed, he calls his doctor. That very day, after tests and sharing his recurring symptoms with the triage nurse, his doctor walks into the examining room, softly closes the door, turns and stops in his tracks: "Richard," he declares in alarm, "your skin has turned yellow with jaundice! By the way, the blood work reveals that your bilirubin is skyrocketing—that's the cause of the uncontrollable itching you're complaining about. Quite simply, we've not a moment to lose: *your entire liver system is shutting down on you.* As soon as you leave, I'll be calling hospital emergency, telling them to expect you within two-hours' time."

"For how long? Uh, what will they do? I . . . uh . . . am meeting some *very important* church leaders tomorrow—" he stops, meeting the doctor's stern gaze.

"Richard, you're not getting my message: This is *serious*! Your very life is at stake—and I have not the slightest idea as to what is causing the jaundice. I can only hope hospital doctors will find out in time. If they don't—" he pauses, at loss for the right words, then concludes with, "just *hurry* . . . and may God be with you!"

Journey by gurney

Two hours later, Richard and Laura arrive at the emergency entrance. After being admitted, he is wheeled into a room Laura later labels "a switching-room" (for he's never in it very long). In this room, he loses his identity and position: once he takes off his clothes and dons one of those drafty, exposing, humiliating hospital gowns that tie (ever so clumsily) in the back, he is no longer the "well-known Dr. Richard J. Moore, pastor of the largest and most prestigious church in the state," but rather he will henceforth be known simply as "Mr. Moore" or more often, "When were you born?" (at all times of the day and night that eternal question will be asked)—to make sure new shifts of nurses and aides administer the right medications to him. Even more humiliating, rarely will his name be used at all! He is just "the patient in room 1211." Over the years, he had visited parishioners in the hospital many times. But that was in the early years before he had a large staff and a "pastor of visitation" to take care of such things. But this was nothing at all like being a visitor!

From this time on, Richard feels like flotsam bobbing up and down in a storm-swollen river—no longer in control of anything! For now he is but a part of a race against time. The goal: keep him alive long enough to find out if there is anything modern medicine can do to stave off death.

For much of the night, his gurney is wheeled down the long corridors to room after room, machine after machine—X-ray and CAT scan among them. When the EKG (electrocardiograph) machine lights up, Richard turns toward it and says to himself, *Oh, I've seen that machine before—on TV and in the movies. Usually, though, when I've seen one, it has to do with a [gulp!] life-or-death situation.* While watching those undulating waves with morbid fascination, he can't help but wonder, *How many times in my life have those waves rolled across like that? And death is neither more nor less than one of those waves going down—but not up—on the other side.* Then the full impact hits him: *That's me on that screen! ME!* Tensely, he begins willing each wave to go up, go down—and then keep going. But finally, *I can't watch anymore: the suspense is just too much,* and he turns away.

Hour after hour, the blur of long hallways; the everlasting harpooning with needles; the blood-pressure checks, the breathing-flow checks; the re-asking of his date of birth; the passing of other gurneys bearing patients just like him; the lights—bright, medium, and low; the variant sounds of machines; the cacophony of speech sounds coming from doctors, nurses, aides, and technicians; the ringing of telephones; the strident voice on the intercom usually calling "Doctor ____";

it all produces a numbness; Richard feels like a laboratory rat that has no say in anything, at the total mercy of Olympians and their machinery.

Meanwhile, Laura has been permitted to trail along behind his many peregrinations—always there'd be a waiting room nearby. She keeps track of every procedure, every test, answers questions (as her husband is, more often than not, in a fog of nonawareness); in short, she is both his protector and advocate. Somewhere in the wee hours of the morning, an empathetic doctor, seeing how exhausted she is, suggests she go home. Gratefully, she takes his advice. With great difficulty, she stays awake during the fifty-mile trip.

Some time later, Richard is wheeled out of emergency and taken upstairs to a hospital room of his own. An IV pole resembling an electronic tree is wheeled over to his bed and tubes of liquids connected so as to bring his sodium levels under control; Benadryl is injected into his bloodstream in order to moderate the raging bilirubin-driven itch—he is now on a totally liquid diet.

This proves to be but the first of a number of nights that grant him precious little rest, for doctors, nurses, aides, and technicians continue to shuttle in and out, and the multitudinous sounds of the hospital never stop; like New York, it is a city that never sleeps. Richard begins dreading pit stops for he has to buzz the night nurse, get partly disconnected, then tow the electronic tree into the bathroom with him; when through making another contribution to the urine jug, it's back to bed and another reconnecting process. Periodically, when he manages to doze off, he'll inadvertently crook his elbow, thus jamming the vein connection and setting off the tree's raucous beeper. The morning shower is even more of a logistical nightmare.

Finally, there is welcome silence in his room—and it remains that way for some time. Until Laura walks in and greets him with a solicitous smile.

He asks, "What time did you get home?"

"Oh, I believe it was close to four o'clock."

"Really? And you're here already—you couldn't have slept more than a couple hours. Why didn't you sleep in?"

"I couldn't. I just felt you might need me."

"Well, I do . . . but you look exhausted."

She says nothing. Neither does he. In that respect, there has been no improvement since the cruise.

Finally, Richard breaks the awkward silence: "It was nonstop most of the night, but this morning—*nothing*! Does anybody at the top even know I'm here? Is there a mastermind in this place? Anybody on first?"

Laura chuckles, "Don't really know, but it sure is quiet."

Silence again. Laura picks up a book and Richard memorizes the walls and ceiling of the room. Then in walks Richard's associate pastor, who's come in for marching orders, both for himself and for the church. "Should we tell them?" he asks.

"Not yet," is the response. "Until we know more, there really is no news to tell."

"Well, you're the boss, but it's sure going to be hard to keep this quiet—and you know how news travels in our congregation. After all, you'll be getting calls on Monday." Shortly afterwards, he leaves, promising to check in each day.

Suddenly, a knock, and in walks a doctor who introduces himself as a hospitalist.

"A *what*?" Richard asks.

"A hospitalist," he repeats. "This is a fairly new position in large hospitals. It is a doctor whose entire job description has to do with assimilating all the data feeding in through machines, tests, samples, nurses, doctors, and surgeons, and making some sense of it all, both for the hospital and for the patient. And I help to keep things moving along."

Marveling, and exhibiting a 180-degree mood swing, Richard says, "I can't believe it. You mean there really *is* someone on first?"

The doctor laughs, saying, "Yes, that's my job. I'm the go-between. I'm the one person who is supposed to make this incredibly complex hospital work. But I'm curious, What do you mean about someone 'being on first'?"

"I'm sorry. I'm just a media buff and sports nut. That line comes from the most famous radio skit ever recorded, Abbott and Costello's legendary baseball skit, 'Who's on First'-base, that is."

"Oh, I get you. Naturally, you've been lying here wondering if we were a hospital jammed with Indians—but no chief in sight."

"Bingo! Just what I was wondering. But Doctor, back to the heart of the matter, what have all these tests revealed? Answers, I hope."

"I'm afraid we don't have any real answers yet. All the relatively uncomplicated possibilities have been explored— and discarded. I really don't think any of us are going to be very happy with the options that remain. We can only hope that the MRI machine will provide answers. If it does not—" he leaves the sentence incomplete.

"But Doctor, you must have *some* idea as to what's so terribly wrong inside me. Some likely probabilities, judging on the basis of the data so far."

"I do—but you really wouldn't want to know."

"Why?"

"Because," and his face reveals some of the inner torment his position generates, "because three out of the five probabilities are too horrible to even share with you at this stage." Then he rises and says, "I'll be back later. We'll talk more then," and leaves.

Neither Richard nor Laura know what to say to each other, for the hospitalist has made it all too clear that the hospital's investigators are fast running out of machines. Thus the MRI machine represents their last best hope: if it fails to reveal why Richard's liver system is shutting down on him, his future is bleak indeed.

Suddenly, another knock. An aide pushes in the largest gurney used yet, and announces that the time has come for another test. This trip—to the three million dollar state-of-the-art MRI machine. After yet another trip down endless hallways, Richard is wheeled into a large room dominated by one imposing piece of medical machinery. He is now shifted from the gurney onto a very narrow and very hard something that is neither a bed nor a marble slab—but something in-between.

Richard stares with more than a little trepidation at the small tunnel he will be entering. It seems so *small*! And it *is* small. He can't help wondering, *Will I even fit in it? What if I get claustrophobia?* Gradually the master of the machine calms Richard down, positions him with strategically placed pillows, and asks him to choose some music—for he's going to be in the belly of this monster for three-quarters of an hour! With a wry sort of a grin, Richard chooses the original soundtrack of *The Phantom of the Opera*. Then Richard's hands are positioned over his head in front of him, for inside there will be no room for them at his side. Indeed, though he isn't told this, once inside he'll be so immobilized he'd be unable to ever get out on his own.

Richard is now told that he will be given commands to "Take a deep breath—hold it—release it!" again and again, for the magnetic resonance imaging will be so distorted as to be worthless, unless he dutifully holds his breath for twenty, twenty-five, even thirty seconds at a time. Finally, he is blindfolded, and feels himself moving.

Once inside, his mind plays such tricks on him that he feels he's inside what seems like miles and miles of tunnels. Suddenly, the sensory overload that is *The Phantom of the Opera* assaults him—but is never permitted to hold center stage alone for more than seconds. For his ears are almost continuously bombarded by every imaginable type of sound: deep ocean liner blasts; trumpet sounds varying from tenor to rumbling sousaphone bass; bell-like tones ranging from wind chimes tinkling to full-throated clanging like Big Ben of London; mournful foghorn laments. It is like being immersed deep in the ocean, and all around, he hears the sounds of whales, seals, porpoises, dolphins, walruses, otters, manatees—all cavorting and speaking to each other (each sound tied to one of those obnoxious commands, "Take a deep breath, hold it, release it"), sometimes holding his breath so long he fears his lungs will burst!

After what seems an eternity, Richard is brought out of the tunnel, his blindfold removed, told to take some deep breaths, and then moved back inside the monster—only this time without the blindfold. He then realizes how grateful he ought to be for the earlier use of the blindfold, for it seems his eyebrows can almost touch the ceiling of the machine. Brief though this second journey is, it's most claustrophobic!

Once released, Richard peppers the master of the machine with questions. In self-defense, the technician agrees to let him see the results for himself. Once the machine has fully digested the forty-five minutes of imaging, the pictures start coming in. Richard is overwhelmed because there, for the first time in his life, he sees, like thin slices of a giant grapefruit, graphic representations of his internal organs, including their proximity and relationship to each other. Flip, flip, flip, flip!—that's *me, me inside*—for all the world (certainly the hospital staff) to see and study! As art, it strikes him as unbelievably beautiful, symmetrical, balanced, and complex. He can't help but marvel at a Creator who could have designed such a masterpiece of engineering!

Reluctantly, Richard leaves this fascinating room and permits himself to be wheeled back to the hospital room where he is reattached to all his tentacles. More doctors, more ministrations by nurses, aides, and technicians. But still no answers. Evening comes, and Laura, unutterably weary and stressed, stands up, leans over to plant a perfunctory kiss on his forehead, then heads home without any words—because there aren't any words.

Some time later, in walks the hospitalist who quietly closes the outer door, pulls the curtain, and takes a chair near Richard's bed. His face is grave—all bantering gone. After a long silence, he clears his throat, and asks, "How honest do you want me to be?" Glibly, Richard answers, "Brutally honest!" After another long silence, the doctor says, "I don't think you really mean that, for the news is not good. The MRI scans reveal that your bile duct is clogged with gallstones and debris—that's why your liver system is shutting down."

"So," Richard answers, struggling for control, "is there no hope?"

"Yes," comes the answer, "there is a procedure we can use that will enable us to send an endoscope (a gadget with a camera, claws, and holding basket) down through your esophagus into the bile duct. Then, in the hands of the best surgeon we can find, the journey of exploration, removal of each obstruction or piece of debris he finds, can take place."

"So what's the problem?" breaks in Richard.

"The problem is that this procedure called ERCP can be relatively safe (of course *any* invasion of anyone's inner space—even including anesthesia—can be risky to a patient). The problem, in your case, is that endoscope must be snaked down to the most dangerous part of your body, where the risk gets higher every inch the endoscope goes."

"But *why*?" Richard counters.

"Because," he pauses again, "you're now entering the realm of the pancreas."

Richard shudders, for the morning before he entered the hospital he finished reading a book that was sweeping the nation, Carnegie Mellon professor Randy Pausch's deeply moving bestseller, *The Last Lecture*. Only forty-seven years old, with a lovely wife and three adorable little children (Logan, Chloe, and Dylan)—so very much to live for—Dr. Pausch was told his liver system was not only shutting down on him, it was full of tumors. Short of a miracle, he'd die of pancreatic cancer within a few months. Regretting most of all the fact that he wouldn't be there for his kids during the rest of their growing up years (the youngest was only eighteen months old) or to grow old with his wife, he decided to pour into a last lecture his entire philosophy of life, ostensibly for his students but really for his children. Shortly after delivering that last lecture, Dr. Pausch died.

Yes, Richard knows what the pancreas is.

The doctor continues, "The problem is this: the closer the endoscope gets to the pancreas, the higher the risk. But the good news is that, in most cases, the procedure takes place without a hitch."

"In *most* cases? Can you be more specific than that?"

"*Yes*—It is successful ninety to ninety-five percent of the time."

"Oh, you're telling me that five to ten of every hundred patients who undergo this procedure—that they—"

Another look of pain in the doctor's eyes. "But Richard, you must balance this risk against the alternative."

"Yes, I know. If we do nothing—it's all but over."

The doctor is silent.

"Doesn't give me many options, does it?"

"No . . . so what is your decision?"

"Don't see that there's much of an alternative. Let's go for it."

The doctor stands up. "Good! We'll assemble a team—it'll be more difficult than normal for we're always shorthanded on Sundays. We'll schedule it first thing in the morning. I'll be in touch." He then pulls the curtain back and leaves.

Epiphany

It is a *very* long night, with sleep being all but impossible. All Richard can initially think about are those stark odds:

Out of every hundred patients like me—five to ten won't. Though he doesn't yet know what that one word *won't* means, what it entails, it still causes him to shudder.

He dares not phone Laura with the grim news. For when words already come difficult, how can he explain the significance of tomorrow's risky procedure to her? If indeed the worst that can happen, does, what then? What if only months, weeks, or days remain to him—to them?

His thoughts stray onto forbidden ground: *It terrifies me to face head-on the very real possibility that, for me, life may be over. I'm far too young for such a thing! We've never even made out a will—"plenty of time for that when we get old." But what if now, we have to?*

One by one, during that interminable night, he objectively reconsiders all his life's priorities.

His career? For the first time in many years he metaphorically takes off his rose-tinted glasses as he looks at himself and his motivations. Is preaching God's word really nothing more than a career to him? A living? Could clawing for power—even religious power—ever be a good thing? What about his lust for ever larger churches, ever larger media audiences? Could such goals be considered admirable? *How would his Lord view them?* Shame, wave after wave rolls in upon him. Here he is, making a living preaching each Sabbath, yet somewhere along the way, he's lost his focus. *I no longer know who it is I'm preaching of! Without this vital connection to God, of what value are my weekly admonitions to the flock? Speaking of which, I haven't cared two cents about the flock God entrusted to me! Doesn't even show up on my radar screen. People have come to bore me, and flocks of people bore me even more. They're little more than a means to ever larger paychecks, ever more laudatory press releases.*

So what would it mean to my church if my life and career were over? Not much. I don't engage their hearts—I only inform them, impress them, entertain them. But, oh God! Now I see! Those things are merely meringue, superficial things that anyone could provide just as well as I—perhaps better. The collective church might hardly miss a beat were I no longer there. Unless my words reach the heart itself and, through God's help, change lives for the better, of what possible value are they? Unless I help to turn listeners into real disciples—which I've failed to do in all too many cases. Then the awful realization, Almost everything I've done and said has been for the glory of Dr. Richard Moore and not for the glory of God!*

Not since the spiritual fervor of his early childhood has Richard experienced such an awakening, such a clear-eyed view of his true spiritual condition. Like a monstrous mansion constructed of defective materials, put together with shoddy workmanship, and constructed on a constantly shifting earthquake fault, the edifice of his dreams now collapses. In the dust clouds of such an implosion, in the shambles he's made of his life and career, Richard finds himself metaphorically on his knees, pleading for God's forgiveness, begging for another chance. Like Jacob who wrestled all night with an Angel, refusing to release him without a blessing, so Richard wrestles all night with God.

Finally, just before dawn, God grants him peace—and Richard sleeps.

The road now taken

About an hour later, hospital noise precluding more sleep than that, Richard awakens to the first day of the rest of his life. He is amazed, in light of all his sleep deprivation, at how energized he feels. How at peace. How excited about life.

Once the news that the ERCP has been postponed until tomorrow (so that a seasoned team will be on deck) reaches him, Richard's thoughts pick up where they left off. He has been a complete failure as a pastor, as shepherd to his Lord's sheep.

* * * * *

Which brings him to his marriage. Laura had phoned earlier, asking for a full report from the hospitalist, and what lay ahead during the day. In capsule-form, he'd given it to her, minimizing the risk factor. Upon learning of the upcoming ERCP and its postponement, there follows an awkward silence.

"A problem with the postponement?" he asks.

"Not at all. It's just that I'm not feeling well. In fact, I'm still in bed. Feel like I've been run over by a truck."

Strangely, Richard finds uncharacteristically solicitous words coming out of his mouth: "Why you poor dear! Of *course* you're exhausted from all this stress. Why don't you just stay in bed and rest today? I'll be fine."

"Really?" Richard can sense disbelief on the other end of the line—surely this can't be the insensitive unempathetic husband she's lived with all these years!

"Really. Hopefully, you'll feel better tomorrow."

"Thank you, Richard—I really do need some rest."

And then he astonishes himself even more: "And Laura—"

"Yes?"

"I just wanted to say . . . uh . . . that I . . . uh—"

"Yes?"

"I . . . uh . . . just wanted to say . . . that I . . . that I . . . love you."

Silence. Unbelieving silence.

"Did I just hear what I thought I heard?"

"Yes . . . I said 'I love you.' "

Silence. "So what's the catch?"

"What do you mean? There's no catch."

"Oh come now, Richard, with you, there's *always* a catch. Always an agenda. It has been years since I've known you to ingratiate yourself with someone without an ulterior motive."

"I know that. And I'm not proud of that. But this time, I'm sincere."

"I don't believe you."

"Well," sighs Richard, "I'm not up to debating anyone today."

"Let me think about it. If I'm up to it, I'll see you tomorrow."

"Good. Now get some sleep—dear."

"I will. Thank you."

As Richard hangs up the phone, he has to fight uncharacteristic remorse: *I've failed as a husband too. I've put Laura on hold for such a very long time—I'd have treated a hired maid with more consideration! In my arrogance, I'd just taken for granted that she'd stay with me for life, no matter how I treated her. After all, she was married to a rising star in our church hierarchy. What a laugh! Where has my mind been all these years? More to the point, where has my heart been?*

Once the logjam of his own egocentricity has broken loose, he's flooded by memories: memories of a beautiful bride, radiant in the conviction that she was unconditionally loved; memories of a young wife who tried to caution him about permitting his growing workaholism to take precedence over their love for each other; memories of the oft-seen pain—even anguish—in her eyes at his growing coldness and belittling remarks.

The many times he'd either forgotten or ignored her birthday or their anniversary. The times when she'd wanted him to go home with her to visit her parents—he'd usually either pressure her to stay home or curtly mutter something such as, "If it means *that* much to you, just *go!*" Half the time, she'd just look at him like a wounded doe, shot by mistake, and resignedly stay home. Lately, her attitude had changed, almost as if she'd given up on him, and was resigned to developing a life of her own. The same pattern was holding true for other getaways, trips, and vacations she'd suggested through the years. Whatever she suggested, he'd pooh-poohed; whatever *he* suggested (almost invariably tied to speaking engagements or opportunities to advance his career), they'd taken. But in recent years, the last time he'd halfheartedly asked if she wanted to go along on such a trip, she'd looked at him with a half-disgusted, half-resigned look in her eyes, and said, "Richard, you don't *really* want me along. You'd rather go alone and preen your feathers in front of your groupies—especially the pretty ones." His face turning ten shades of red, he'd said nothing, recognizing the truth in her words—just turned on his heels without a word, slammed the door behind him to show what he thought of her, and stalked off in high dudgeon to the church office.

So now, using funds bequeathed to her by her maternal grandmother, she'd ceased to even ask him to go with her, and would go by herself or with a close friend or relative. Until this moment, he'd thought nothing of it; brushed it off,

just as he'd brushed her off for so many years. But not now. As Laura's last words were still reverberating in his mind, his mind veered into a totally new channel. *I'm an unmitigated fool! Laura is still lovely, still turns heads. What's to keep her from finding someone else now that she's apparently given up on me! What have I done!*

* * * * *

Something else happened to Richard during his night struggle with God. All his life, he'd been self-centered with skewed priorities. But now that his inner center of gravity has shifted, something other than self must fill the vacuum. Richard is himself amazed at his sudden interest in both the day shift and the night shift, and his compulsion to ask each person questions, such as, "So where did you come from originally?" "What brought you here?" "As to your work here in the hospital, do you enjoy it?" "I imagine things can get pretty hectic around here." "Have a family?" If so, inquiring about them. And the real shocker, "So what do you plan to do with the rest of your life?"

Amazingly, during those sometimes interminable night hours when fewer intrusions arise, night nurses, aides, technicians, even doctors, respond to such questions enthusiastically. Almost as though inwardly each was thinking, *This man perceives me not merely as another piece of hospital machinery—but as a real person! One who also has frustrations, concerns, struggles, questions, and family.* Night doctors look at Richard almost in disbelief, so used are they to being considered omniscient medical gods rather than human beings with their own needs, insecurities, and dreams. They lean back

and talk and talk, patently reluctant to leave an experience so rare in their medical practice.

* * * * *

Several days will pass before Richard fully realizes what has been happening to him. God has replaced his erstwhile self-centeredness with a passion for His sheep. For truly Christ's entire earthly ministry had virtually nothing in it about creed, but *everything* about selfless service to those in need. Hence the life-changing realization: *only in selfless service to others may life be worth living.*

The next afternoon, Richard is wheeled into an operating room, put under anesthesia, and knows nothing until several hours later when he begins to be groggily aware of blurred figures around him. Clearly pleased, the surgeon informs him that they were successful in retrieving seven gallstones in the bile channel. Eventually, providing there are no unforeseen complications elsewhere, the bilirubin-induced itch should slacken off and finally cease. If everything still looks good tomorrow, the decision as to what should be done about the gallbladder can be made then. But, there remains an anything but small *if.* If at any time during the night, Richard should begin to experience the most excruciating pain a human being can endure, it will signal the horrible news that pancreatitis has set in. "You don't even want to know how terrible it can be!"

Then Richard is wheeled back to his room. He gives Laura the good news and downplays the terrors of the upcoming night. There will be time enough tomorrow, if worst comes to worst, to prepare for the end.

As his eyes take in Laura sitting on a chair by the window, a pensive look on her face, he wonders what she's thinking about. Also, he really *sees* her, for the first time since the earliest years of their marriage. For years now, she's merely been part of the woodwork, the faithful servant who could be counted on to minister to his day-to-day needs and demands. But now—*true, she's beautiful in feature and form, but now I know how beautiful she is inside. That tender heart I've taken for granted—no, far worse than that: I've ruthlessly trampled on it! Because we've grown so far apart, we can't even talk about what's ahead—my fears.*

It turns out to be the longest and most aging night of Richard's life, for each new breath he takes could bring that horrible first swordthrust of pain. He prays a lot—almost unceasingly. He thanks God for the gift of life, then humbly asks that if it should be His will, that he be granted additional life "so that I may begin to make up to my congregation and my wife, all that I have heretofore deprived them of."

When the stress gets to be almost more than flesh and blood can stand, Richard—finally unshackled from his electronic tree—walks the halls in a vain attempt to keep his mind from fixating on that next breath.

Midnight finds him in the break room where he grabs a snack—it seems forever since he has been able to eat anything. Shortly after he sits down, a woman in her eighties walks in, and not seeing anyone else there besides Richard, asks if she may join him. They strike up a conversation. Turns out her husband is in a room just down the hall. No, he's not the one who yells out in the middle of the night, "Let me out of here!" or "Help!" but he's next door so there's no escaping that poor man's ravings. She continues, "My husband has a virulent form of leukemia."

117

Casually, Richard responds, "Oh? How long has he had it?"

"Twenty-five years."

"Twenty-five years!"

Wearily, she adds, "Yes, twenty-five long years. And I have been his nurse every day of that time. In fact, he can't even turn over without my help."

Almost in shock at such almost unheard of devotion, Richard says, "My dear woman, how do you *do* it without cracking, year after year?"

Never would Richard forget her response: "Oh, it's not that hard—for the good Lord gives you just enough strength for *one day at a time.*" At that, all barriers between the two splinter, and Richard finds himself telling her that he's on a prayer vigil because this might very well be the last pain-free night of his lifetime. The two then commune with each other until around 2:00 A.M. They then hold hands, each praying for the other; then she returns to her husband's pain-wracked room, and Richard to his pacing the hallways—praying, hoping. Shortly after 4:00 A.M., sleep deprivation so overcomes Richard that he falls asleep on his bed.

Several hours later, when he awakens to a new day, oh the joy that floods through him when the realization hits him: I AM TO LIVE! It will be several days before a surgeon in California tells him just what it was that he averted. "The pancreas is the seething cauldron of your body. In it, the cholesterol and fat taken into the body are broken down so that your digestive system may continue to do its job. But if a particle should be dislodged—say by a searching endoscope—and escape into the bile duct, putting it mildly, all hell will break loose! The pancreas will go crazy in rage, and immediately begin to devour itself (cannibalize itself, if you will). In most cases, the all but doomed patient will experience sixty to ninety days of the most excruciating pain a human being can endure before, in mercy, it will be over." No wonder the hospitalist considered pancreatitis too horrible to even explain to him!

Several hours after being wheeled back to his room, Richard hears a familiar knock, and "Anybody home?"

"Come in, Dr. H. Been looking for you."

The hospitalist takes the usual chair. "Dr. H. What's the *H* for—the fact that I'm a hospitalist?"

"Yes. And the fact that you're a harbinger."

"Ah *what?*"

"Harbinger, a messenger who lets me know what's going to hit me next."

Muttering goodnaturedly, "You and your big words. By the way, I was able to run down a recording of Abbott and Costello's 'Who's on First.' Haven't laughed so hard in years. I'll have to pick up some of their other comedies.

"Switching gears, it's good to see you made it through the night."

"Yes," says Richard gratefully, *"I'm to live!"*

"We do some things right—of course you had a good surgeon, the best in the city. So now we can discuss the next step. The ultrasound results just came in. They're inconclusive. There may be gallstones lurking inside—we can't really tell. Even so, that's the only place in the body where gallstones are made."

"In other words, more are likely to be made."

"Precisely. With the attendant risk that they may stray into the bile duct."

"Don't think I could handle that twice in one lifetime. And I understand I can get along OK without the gallbladder."

"Yes. Untold thousands appear to have no significant side effects, though some have to alter their diet a bit."

"In that case, while I'm here I'd just as soon finish the job, so I can go on with my life."

"Very good. I've already checked with the top gallbladder surgeon I know. He can do the surgery Friday. Today it's so noninvasive—three slits in your chest—that, barring complications, you may be able to go home by evening."

"Let's do it."

The doctor gets up to go, stares at the empty chair by the window, and says, "By the way, haven't seen your beautiful leading lady for a while. She was *always* here earlier on. Is she ill?"

Clearly uncomfortable with the question, Richard hesitates, then says, "Well, yes and no. Yes, that she hasn't felt good; no, in that there's more to it than that."

"Oh, sorry. I didn't mean to intrude on your private business."

"No, no. It's just that we haven't been getting along very well for some time."

A quizzical look appears in Dr. H's eyes, and he asks, "Is she on first in your life?" Noting Richard's stunned reaction, he continues, "The reason I'm asking is that I'm a workaholic, and am rarely home. Practically live at the hospital. My wife was definitely not on first."

"*Was?*" Richard asks, almost in a whisper.

"*Was*, and earlier this year, she just plain gave up on me. Left me. I'm still trying to win her back, but I wouldn't say my odds were very good. I neglected her far too long. That's why

I butted in where I had no business going, and asked you that question."

"Well, to tell you the truth, Doctor, Laura has *not* been on first in my life for a mighty long time—I, too, am a workaholic. It very well may be too late for me as well."

* * * * *

On Friday, the operation to remove the gallbladder is a success. By midevening Richard is able to check out, and Laura drives him home. But all is not well: his body refuses to retain either liquids or solids, expelling them with violence. So several days later, Laura once more drives him down to the hospital, where he is readmitted. Richard wonders, *Could it be that I've come this far only to discover that it was a terrible mistake to remove the gallbladder? What if I can't live without it?*

Fortunately, the hospital staff is able to stabilize the warring elements in Richard's body. Midmorning Tuesday, a familiar knock, and "Anybody home?"

Again the hospitalist sits down by the bed, then smiles. "I hear you've made it through this one too—let's hope the third time's a charm. Unless you're ready to make this room your permanent home, I imagine you'd just as soon go home." Turning to the window, he continues, "How about you, Mrs. Moore? Tired of being a taxi driver?"

"Afraid so," she answers wearily. "Afraid so."

"Well," standing up, "within two hours, when your release comes through, you're free to go. It's been special getting to know you, Richard. Don't often become personal friends with my patients—but with you it has been different."

"The same with me," says Richard, reaching out to shake his hand. "In fact, I'd like to stay in contact. We have . . . uh . . . much in common."

"Let's do it! Goodbye—and goodbye to you too, Mrs. Moore."

And he walks out of the room—wondering.

Intermezzo

Gradually, Richard recovers, his strength and stamina returning all too slowly. But each day, he feels stronger. Within three weeks, he has been able to resume his leadership at the church. But it is the home front that worries him now. No matter how many times he tells Laura he loves her, she refuses to believe him, saying, "So why should I believe you *now*?"

He has changed his habits: helping her in the house, helping in the yard upkeep, even in the shopping and auto maintenance. All to no avail. Surprising himself, knowing how self-sufficient he's always been, he seeks out the most beloved Christian counselor he knows and asks for guidance. In telling the story of his marriage, he frankly acknowledges that the fault is all his. Indeed, it's a wonder Laura didn't leave him long ago! The counselor is wise, knowing that, with such provocation, healing is not likely to come quickly—if it comes at all. He gives Richard reading assignments each week.

Several months after leaving the hospital for the last time, Richard takes Laura out to eat. Once seated in one of the quietest alcoves of the restaurant, Laura asks him, "Richard, why did you bring me here? You've known it was my favorite restaurant for many years now, yet you'd never agree to bring me here. Why *now*?"

After struggling for the right words, Richard answers, "I know you won't believe me, but I brought you here because I love you and want above all things to make you happy."

"That won't wash with me! You haven't given two hoots about making me happy for years and years now." After a long silence, she continues, "Richard, look at me and tell me the honest truth. Why did you marry me?"

Blindsided by such a question out of the blue, Richard stumbles with his words, "Well . . . uh . . . since you . . . uh . . . asked for the 'honest truth,' because you were the most beautiful woman in three counties."

"Oh," Laura answers, clearly disappointed. "Well, at least you're honest. So what happens when my looks go—do I go too?"

Shamed beyond belief, Richard answers, "No, because I've now fallen in love with that great heart inside you. The heart that I've inexcusably trampled on all these years. I make no excuses for how I've treated you, I'm only brazen enough to beg for another chance—so I can spend the rest of our lives proving to you that I'm a changed man."

"Changed? How? By what?"

"By what happened to me at the hospital. By the conviction that my body was falling apart, that unless a miracle occurred, my race was over—"

"*That* changed you?" Unbelief expressed in every word.

"That, and what I've been trying to tell you for months now—I found God."

"You hadn't found Him before? Preposterous! You're a preacher. It's almost . . . uh . . . sacrilegious to admit you preached about God all these years without finding God in the first place."

"Yet, it's true," admits Richard miserably. "I knew God once, when I was a child, but somewhere along the way, as my ego shoved God out of my life, I just plain lost Him."

For the first time, Laura's face softens somewhat. "Strangely enough, even though I don't want to believe you, I think you're telling me the truth this time."

Richard is inspired to go on the counterattack, "Laura, I know I have no right to ask this, but I really, truly want to know. What do *you* want to do with the rest of your life? Say I wasn't even in the picture, surely you have unfulfilled dreams."

Wonderingly, Laura ponders the question, before answering, "If . . . you . . . were . . . out of the picture, I'd travel. I'd take cruises. I'd take classes in lots of subjects. I'd visit art galleries and museums. I'd get to know the people I met, both here and abroad. I'd walk beaches early in the morning and during the moonlight. I'd hike high into the mountains. I'd learn new things every day. But I'm . . . not selfish. I'd want to help people better their lives, I'd want to make a difference. Leave the world a better place than it was had I never been. As for a place to live, I'd leave our palatial home in a heartbeat. I'd like a rustic cabin in the mountains by a stream that will sing lullabies to me at night, and I'd like a place on or near a beach where I can hear the waves crashing in. I'd want to do crazy unexpected things whenever the mood hit me—every day an adventure!" She stops in confusion.

Richard smiles, almost overwhelmed by this explosion of unarticulated dreams. Then he adds, "But what if I *were* in the picture?"

"But you aren't, Richard! You know that. You're too full of Dr. Richard J. Moore and the adulation of the crowds. It's just your way. You may *say* you've changed, but nothing can convince me that you have. You just want—as you always have—to have it all. I'm a convenience, an enabler, you'd rather not do without. But as to really *loving* me, I don't believe that for a second! You're way too selfish to ever really put me and my dreams ahead of yours. Case closed. What shall we order?"

The clock of life

The vast church is so full ushers are having to bring in folding chairs. Since Richard's recovery, *everything* has changed. The pastor most of all. Most church members appear happy about these changes, but a significant number are not—and have been vocal about it. They are the ones who like their church to be a combination of a country club for the wealthy and an entertainment center for those who have little interest in selfless service for others. Yet a majority, slim though it be, are intrigued by their pastor's simple approach to the gospel and his new interest in *every* member of the congregation.

For weeks now, speculation has been building about what it is that the pastor is going to preach about this Christmas. Indeed, the wildest rumors are rampant. All anyone knows for sure is that it will be dramatic—and that alone is enough to bring in even those who are members in name only.

The great church (in appearance more like a stadium than a traditional house of worship) is decorated beautifully but far more simply than normal for a Christmas service.

Usually the Christmas service in Moore's church is a spectacular production. Dramatic with plenty of well-known musical performers to validate the importance of the church. But not so this year. Quietly, Richard walks to the center of the platform—there is no pulpit this Christmas—and begins to speak.

"Beloved family—this is Christmas, the season young and old cherish more than any other. Not because of an orgy of present exchanges, but because it is the season of the Christ Child.

"The title of my thoughts for today is not listed in the bulletin. Indeed, it is a rather strange title for a Christmas sermon—'The Clock of Life.' As many of you know, during the last fifteen months, my liver system gradually began shutting down on me. It was in early September when my beloved wife, Laura," and here he fondly looks down at her, "accompanied me to the hospital."

Briefly, Richard sketches out for his listeners what it was like for a workaholic like himself to suddenly lose control of every aspect of his life. The congregation leans forward in fascination, for this intimate sharing of his life is so foreign to the sermons he's preached before. Eventually, he gets back to the sermon title.

"On the wall above my hospital bed was a large clock, and its hands moved very very slow. I know, because I had little else to stare at. There on that bed, for the first time ever, I really became aware of the fragility of life. For I'd been informed by my attending physician that unless they were able to find out what was shutting down my liver system—*quickly*, for my skin had already turned yellow with jaundice—my life's

course was all but run. And if they discovered the cause in time, the next question would be, Could anything be done about it?

"Later in the week, they *did* discover the cause, and they *did* go inside me to deal with that cause. But that prowling around in the general vicinity of the pancreas involved a frightening risk that, in the process, I would become a victim of pancreatitis (and my doctor refused to even tell me how horrible that could be).

"In short, I never knew from one moment to the next whether or not I'd be with you—or with Laura—this Christmas, for the clock of my life was remorselessly ticking away and I had no way of knowing at what particular moment it might stop.

"During one of those traumatic nights, I experienced a life-changing epiphany. Given that I now realized my life might be at its terminus, I reshuffled all my life's priorities. It is sobering to realize how radically priorities change when life itself is at stake! Suddenly, money, position, prestige, fame, travel, houses, automobiles, and possessions mean absolutely nothing—when weighed in the balances against life itself.

"Had you been in my place, you would have been irrevocably changed by the experience. I certainly have been. I am not the man I was before that life-changing night. Quite candidly, when I took off my rose-tinted glasses and looked at my life and actions through clear lenses, I did not like what I saw.

"I now invite each of you to imagine this Christmas that you, too, have reached what may very well be the last few days of your life. The clock of your life may have reached one minute to twelve—and counting. You have no idea as to whether the hands may stop at twelve for all time—or whether, in God's great mercy, as with me, the hands may continue to move, providing another chance to serve others. For each of us—not just those paid to preach—are shepherds, ministering shepherds.

"I now share with you the poem that has helped to change my life. Copies are available as you go out. I've never found out who the author is.

The Clock of Life

The clock of life is wound but once,
And no one can tell you just when the hands will stop
At late or early hour;
Now is the only time you have;
Live, love, toil with a will;
Place no confidence in tomorrow
For the clock may then be still.

"But for me, this poem has propelled me into a life-changing decision. Laura, would you be so kind as to join me on the platform?" After she joins him, unable to figure out a reason for such an unusual request on his part, he continues. "The church board has agreed, albeit reluctantly, to grant my request to leave this pulpit, this church ministry [a collective gasp from the audience] in order to embark on another journey to help out churches struggling to stay alive in these hard times. Chances are some will be unable to pay a minister's salary, however modest; it will make no difference to me. In truth, after being convicted in the hospital that I had all but lost my way spiritually, I want to start all over again, to rebuild my relationship with the Lord. I have much to make up for."

Now he turns to Laura, and it's almost like he's re-saying his marriage vows: "Laura, during the last twenty-one years, I have inexcusably shortchanged you, I have hurt you, I have neglected you. Because of this I have a new proposal for you, Laura Wilson Moore, I am offering you the opportunity to serve with me as my partner in this journey, in which we will travel to churches in need of pastoral assistance, wherever they may be, in America and abroad, and there serve until that church is able to carry on without us. We will have no travel allowance so we will have to be frugal. Fortunately, we have money put aside and royalties from my books. In my preaching, I will start over again, seeking to know my Master as I've never known Him before.

"But Laura, service for the Lord's sheep is only half of my proposal to you. In gratitude for all the ways you enrich my life, I offer you trips on land and sea; art galleries, concert halls, antique stores, old book stores, and museums; a cabin in the mountains with a stream flowing by to sing you to sleep and a modest place near the ocean where you can hear the waves come in and where you can walk the beach in the morning mists and in the gloaming and moonlight. I offer you a full-time husband who will love and cherish you to the limit of every day and every night, a love strengthened by daily prayer and meditation. Laura Wilson Moore, if I promise all this—and I do—would you be willing to sign back on for the rest of our life's journey?"—and he holds his breath, for her answer will dramatically alter the rest of their lives.

He needn't have worried. Those close enough to see saw glory in her eyes, love returning at full strength that had been all but lost in the flotsam of the years. Saw the tender laughter—so long absent—trembling on her lips.

But they'd never have heard what she said to him had not the soundman inexcusably left the microphone on.

Very softly, so the audience had to strain in order to hear, "Richard, dearest, have I ever told you how very much I love you?" And then (all but smothered by his tenderly and thankfully taking her into his arms), half laughter and half sob:

"When do we leave?"

* * * * *

And it was Christmas Day.

About this story

As I proofed the galleys for this story, I was strongly impressed that I should not send it back to my editor without adding an "About this story." Since I made these edits a matter of prayer, I'm convinced it is God's will that I do so. Perhaps my sharing some pages out of my personal journey may make a difference in yours. I can only pray that it will be so.

I short, this story—so uncharacteristic of my previous ones—did not just come to me out of the blue. Except for the lead characters—Richard and Laura—virtually everything in this story happened to me and my wife, Connie, during the last two and a half years. And this includes the cruise to Alaska and West Coast and the bouts of illness that began on board the ship and continued intermittently until last September when my physician gave me two hours in which to check in at the hospital's emergency room. All that happened to Richard in the hospital happened first to me—not excluding the midnight encounter with that woman who for twenty-five years had faithfully remained at her husband's side day and night.

Most of the thoughts that came to Richard came to me as well. *Is my life over? Am I at peace with God? Are my life's key priorities skewed? How large does Self loom in my life? Is ministering to the Lord's sheep first in my life? What about my family, my wife, our children—have I taken them for granted?*

Indeed, I can testify that looking across that hospital bed to the window where my lovely wife, Connie, sat hour after hour, even when clearly exhausted, gave me a new appreciation for all she means to me, and her continuing love.

And it should come as no surprise that each precious day

that followed has been valued far more than those that pre-ceded that Alaskan cruise. For I'm convicted that I'm living on gifted time, that, for some reason known only to Him, God concluded that He wasn't through with me yet—that there was a reason I wasn't one of the five to ten of every hundred who "didn't."

One of the dearest friends life has brought me, Dr. James Dobson of Focus on the Family, phoned me after I got out of the hospital. During that long chat he said, "Joe, I, too, have walked the halls of a hospital in the middle of the night, won-dering if my life's journey was over, if God's plan for my life had reached full circle."

It is a very small club we belong to: those who reach the very brink of eternity—then are pulled back with a reprieve. But the purpose of writing this story is to appeal to all those who have yet to experience what we did—to urge them to live each day as though it were the last day of their lives.

This is my prayer.